BEYOND DREAMS

To Judy -
I hope these stories ring
true to you - Thanks for
ideas - Marilyn

Other Titles in the
True-to-Life Series from Hamilton High
by Marilyn Reynolds:

Too Soon For Jeff

Detour for Emmy

Telling

BEYOND DREAMS

True-to-Life Series
from Hamilton High

By Marilyn Reynolds

Morning
Glory
Press

Buena Park, California

Library of Congress Cataloging-in-Publication Data

Reynolds, Marilyn, 1935-
     Beyond dreams : true-to-life series from Hamilton High /
by Marilyn Reynolds.
          p.   cm.
     Summary: Includes six short stories that deal with crisis
situations faced by teenagers, including racism, abuse, sense
of failure, aging relatives, drunk driving, and abortion.
     ISBN 1-885356-01-3 (hardcover). -- ISBN 1-885356-00-5
(quality paper)
     1. Short stories, American. [1. High schools--Fiction.
2. Schools--Fiction.   3. Short stories.]   I. Title.
     PZ7.R3373Re   1995
     [Fic]--dc20   95-17802
                                                         CIP
                                                          AC

MORNING GLORY PRESS, INC.
6595 San Haroldo Way   Buena Park, CA 90620-3748
(714) 828-1998   FAX (714) 828-2049
Printed and bound in the United States of America

CONTENTS

ACKNOWLEDGMENTS

For taking the time to read and hear these stories in progress, and for offering gently helpful comments, I want to thank:

My writing/critiquing colleagues, particularly Karen Kasaba and Anne Scott.

Barry Barmore and the students at Century High School, especially Alyssa Phu and Tina Ybarra.

Assorted San Gabriel High School students in Donna Potts' Advanced Placement Biology classes, Michael Donnelly's Peer Counseling classes, and Michael Reynolds' chorus classes, especially Catherine Nguyen, Casey Huynh, and San San Ung. Also, from the San Gabriel High School staff, Hoi Vinh, Karen Carrillo, Carol Schneider, and Michelle Buchicchio have been particularly helpful with this project.

All the folks who comprise the spirit of Morning Glory Press.

To Ashley Nicole DiFalco Foncannon
and Kerry Ryan Foncannon

Like Marilyn Reynolds' novels, *Beyond Dreams*
is part of the **True-to-Life Series from Hamilton High.**
Hamilton High is a fictional, urban, ethnically mixed
high school somewhere in Southern California.
Characters in the stories are imaginary
and do not represent specific people or places.

Only If You Think So

Sometimes I wonder if life's even worth the effort.
Things keep getting worse and worse.

1

Here I am at Sojourner High School. Except for the American flag and the California Bear hanging from the flagpole, this place doesn't even look like a school. There are seven classrooms in those metal buildings schools use when they run out of real buildings. Except this school doesn't have any regular buildings. It's all made out of metal. A school for losers my dad calls it. Not that old Gilbert's such a winner himself, sitting home watching TV while he collects his state disability checks. He's the full-of-shit loser—he couldn't even hold on to his wife.

I sit outside the counseling office, waiting to find out what my classes will be. I'm not feeling very good about things right now. Since the eighth grade my life's been headed toward the garbage pit—my dad lost his job, my mom and sister left us, and my best friend moved away. Besides that, I was always in trouble at school, I got kicked off the baseball team, and just last week I was kicked out of Hamilton High School. Sometimes I wonder if life's even worth the effort. Things keep getting worse and worse.

Finally, after about ten minutes of waiting, this old guy comes to the door. He's got gray hair, but long, like down past his shoulders. He's wearing hippie sandals that look like they walked the grounds of the original Woodstock. He motions me into his office. I sit on a hard, brown plastic chair. He sits in a comfortable-looking upholstered chair behind a desk piled with papers, books, dirty coffee cups, and a dying plant. There's a big glass bowl filled with what at first I think is foil wrapped candy, but then I see that it's a bunch of condoms.

"I'm Mr. Grant, the counselor here. Welcome to Sojourner High School," he says. He nods toward the condom-filled bowl, which is still holding my attention. "We're trying to do our bit to combat teen pregnancy—help yourself anytime you want. They're free."

That's another thing that's not great about my life right now. I'm not needing condoms. But if I did I'd buy my own. Considering the quality of school lunches, I sure wouldn't trust the quality of a school condom.

Mr. Grant hands me a packet of stuff about the school.

"Look this over," he says. "Pay close attention to the rules. No gang attire, no fighting, no drugs or alcohol. Any of these things *will* get you kicked out of school. If you come to school possessing or under the influence of any controlled substance the police *will* be called and you *will* be arrested. The same thing is true if you're caught carrying a weapon. Any questions?"

I don't say anything.

"Remember, this is a last chance for you. You either get your act together here or the Hamilton Heights Unified School District washes its hands of you . . . I assume you want to graduate?"

I nod.

"Well, you can do that at Sojourner High. We'll do everything we can to help you. Do your part by getting here every day and staying out of trouble." Then, his voice going deep like he's giving me some heavy wisdom, he says, "It's up to you— basically, that's it."

Basically, I think, it's the same old school shit I've been hearing all my life. Follow the rules, do what we tell you, be a little school-boy robot. Boring.

The truth is, I don't much care if I graduate or not. I'm so far behind in credits right now, I don't think I'll ever catch up. What's the big deal about a high school diploma, anyway? All I ever wanted to do in high school was play baseball, get noticed by a scout, make my way to the Dodgers' dugout. But after the tenth grade my grade point average was so low I was disqualified from the team. Coach Hernandez used to lecture me all the time about keeping my grades up.

"I know you're not stupid," he'd say. "And you're one of the best ball players I've ever had. So how about getting it together? Put your heart in it."

Finally he stopped lecturing. I guess he gave up on me. Last week I stopped by baseball practice to tell him I'd been transferred to Sojourner. He just gave me a long, sad look and shook his head. Then he patted me on the shoulder, wished me luck, and ran back out to the pitcher's mound.

"C'mon guys, this is a tough game we've got coming up. Give it some heart, will you?"

I thought about all the times the coach had told me to give it some heart, or to put my heart in it, meaning to get serious about school *and* baseball. But I don't know. Sometimes I think I don't have any heart. As much as I wanted to play baseball, I couldn't hang with all those full-of-shit classes.

The guy who's the main pitcher for Hamilton High isn't as good as I am. He's okay in the field but he can't hit anything smaller than a basketball. Me, I've got a great arm. That's not being conceited, either. Anyone who's ever seen me play will say I can really pitch. And I can hit better than almost anyone else on the team. But they're playing and I'm not. Oh, well.

I walk into room three—English, my program card says. There are no desks, just big tables like they had in the art room back at Hamilton High. There are only about twelve students sitting at the tables, reading, writing, flipping through magazines. Two kids are on beanbag chairs, reading. I recognize one of them. It's Mark Carlson. I remember him from woodshop.

He was always stoned. One day Henry, one of the school narcs, came and got Mark from class and that's the last I saw of him until today.

I think Mark was dusted when they took him away that day because he had that Frankenstein kind of walk thing, like there was no gravity under his feet. Man, I don't mess with that shit. I may smoke a little weed now and then, but I don't ever want to do the moonwalk.

A gray-haired lady gets up from one of the tables and walks over to me. I hand her my program card and tell her, "I'm new here."

"I'm old here," she says.

That's kind of obvious to me, but I don't say that. Honestly, so far every adult I've seen around here has gray hair. At least at Hamilton High there were some teachers who might live to see the turn of the century.

"I'm Claudia Merton," she says. "Sit wherever you'd like. I'll be over in a minute to get you started on something."

I sit at the end of the first table, kind of away from everyone else.

"Hey, Merton. I need homework," this kid at another table says. He doesn't look like a kiss ass. In fact, for all of Mr. Grant's talk about no gang attire, this guy looks like he just got in from a drive-by shooting—he's wearing pants that are about a size sixty and his jacket's big enough to hold a whole arsenal of automatic weapons.

"Okay, Sam. I'll be with you as soon as I can."

"You forgot yesterday," he says.

"I know. I'm sorry, I just got busy."

"Well, I need it," he whines.

Is this Sam guy gonna cry if he doesn't get homework? What is this, anyway? It'd be a cold day in hell before you'd hear me begging for homework.

"I need homework, too, Merton," a girl says.

It's funny. I've heard there are fights here every day, and drug deals and drive-bys. I heard a guy was killed here last year. I wouldn't admit it to anyone, but I was kind of scared to come to this school. Sojourner's rep does *not* include kids sitting around begging for homework.

Finally the teacher comes over. She sits down beside me. Weird. She asks me what I like to read. Really weird.

"I don't read," I tell her.

"Don't, or can't?" she asks.

"Don't."

"Well, that's how you get credit in this class—reading and writing."

She explains a system where I can get as much or as little credit as I work for. "You get credit or you don't. It's up to you how much."

More of that it's up to you shit. *They* make the rules. *They* hand out the grades, and then they tell you it's up to you. If it was up to me, I'd be out of here.

"Write at least a page a day in your journal," she says, handing me a little notebook like the kind you can buy at Thrifty's. "Write from the heart, about anything you choose. Then find something that interests you to read. I'll show you some things you might like to try," she says.

I sit staring at the notebook. I'm supposed to write a whole page? She's got to be kidding. I write my name on the front of the notebook, open it to the first page, and then sit watching the lines on the paper.

I don't know what to write. How am I supposed to know what to write? I may leave after this period—come back tomorrow. It's not really like school, anyway.

When the teacher finishes arranging homework for Sam and the other student who, I guess, don't have anything else to do after school but homework, she comes over and sits down beside me again. She makes me nervous.

"Can't think of anything to write?"

I nod my head.

"Here's a folder to keep your work in," she says. "Be sure to put your name on it."

"Hey, Merton," Mark yells from his beanbag chair against the opposite wall, "when're you going to the bookstore again?"

"Tomorrow afternoon."

"Don't forget my book," he says.

I glance over at Mark to see if he's for real. I didn't even know he could read.

The teacher gets up and checks a clipboard on the wall. "The new Stephen King book is what you want. Right?"

"Right."

"Only if it's in paperback," she says.

"Well if it's not, get *The Shining*. I haven't read that one yet."

"Okay," she says, then walks back to where I'm sitting. At least this time she doesn't sit down. She hands me a list of possible writing topics.

"Keep this in your folder. It may give you some ideas. For now, choose something from the first five possibilities, unless you've suddenly come up with something. Or better still, just tell me a little bit about yourself on this first page. Is there anything I should know about you? Write whatever comes into your head. Don't worry about spelling." She smiles, then walks over to check on this other guy who probably also has blank pages in his journal.

She wants me to write from my heart? Whatever comes into my head? She wonders if there's anything she should know about me? I start.

One thing you should know about me is that I think school is a bunch of horse shit. School is boring. Reading is boring. I don't like when teachers sit next to me because it makes me nervous. I wouldn't even be here today except my dad says he'll take my car away if I don't come to school every day. He's full of shit, too, but the car's in his name, so what can I do? Even though I paid for it with my own money, from working, it's in his name because I'm a minor. That sucks!

In fact, it's all fucked up.

I wonder what old Merton will do when she reads this. Well, I wrote a page. That's what she wanted, isn't it? Probably she'll freak out when she gets to the last line. I don't give a rat's ass. I've been kicked out of better schools than this one.

Second period is science, room six. One thing I'll say for Sojourner, you don't get tired walking from one class to the next.

"Hey, Dude. Didn't you used to go to Hamilton?"

It's Mark, the moonwalker guy.

"Yeah . . . How long you been here?" I ask.

"I got here first period, just before you," he says.

"No. I mean, how long have you been coming to school here?" I explain. I think maybe he's lost a bunch of brain cells. It seems like it.

"Oh. I been here since before Christmas," he says.

"You going back to Hamilton?"

"Nah. I like it here. It's sad in the girl department, but otherwise it's cool."

I look around. I think he's right about the girls. I don't care. Girls are just trouble, anyway.

For science I was expecting microscopes and lab tables. Instead it's this rank-smelling room with hamsters, rats, fish, snakes, turtles, all kinds of stuff in cages, aquariums, whatever. This is science?

The teacher, Mr. Fowler, looks kind of familiar to me. Maybe he eats at McDonald's or something. He hands me a packet of stuff to do for physical science and tells me there are lots of ways I can earn extra credit if I want to work with the animals, or on special projects they do around the school or in the community. I don't really care about extra credit. I guess I could use some, if I cared about graduating—which I don't.

"You can clean out under the rabbit cages," he says, pointing out the window to this giant pile of crap. "There's the tool," he says, nodding toward a broad, short handled shovel in the corner of the room.

"No, thanks," I say.

"Extra credit and all you can eat," he says, laughing.

"Nope," I say, looking down at the packet on my desk. I start writing the answers to some of the questions, trying to be invisible because I don't know anyone in here, when I get a glimpse of movement out of the corner of my eye. I can't believe it! This girl is sitting at the next table with a big boa constrictor draped over her shoulders, like it's one of those shawl things. I'm not even that crazy about little garden snakes and this thing is huge. I quick look back down at my paper.

I hope no one's seen me staring because if they have, if they know I'm scared, they'll probably wrap that thing around *my* neck. I keep looking at my paper, but I can't concentrate on anything except that there's a killer snake about ten feet away from me. The teacher is talking to some guys over by the computer. He doesn't seem to care that there's a killer snake on the loose. God!

The girl with the snake is getting up now and walking around the room. Everybody else looks real casual. I hope I do, too. I can feel my heart pounding in my chest. She walks over to a big glass cage, unwraps the snake and puts him in it. I begin to breathe again.

My last class is computers. Another gray-haired teacher— Miss Keyes. Unbelievable—she teaches typing and computers and her name is Keyes? But it's a cool class. I like fooling around with computers and I never got to at Hamilton. Only the little school-boys and school-girls got to use them there.

2

When I get home my dad's in front of the TV watching some talk show about women who leave their husbands for other women. My dad used to be a cop, but then something happened—he got rough with a guy he was arresting—broke his arm. So now he's out on a stress leave, watching TV for life—talk shows, soap operas, cooking shows, ancient reruns—anything but the cop shows he always used to watch.

Things were different when my mom was still here. We always had milk and cereal and fruit, and plenty of other stuff I took for granted then, but I miss now—including my mom. She took my little sister, Katie, with her when she went to stay with my grandma. She'd had it with old Gilbert. I don't blame her—he's the number one butthole of the universe. I wish she'd taken me with her, though. We talk on the phone every week, but it's not enough. Why does the boy always get stuck staying with the dad?

That's how it is with my friend, Scott, too. His dad's about as screwed up as mine is. Scott and I used to go to the park all the time in the afternoons. He'd let me practice pitching as long as I wanted. He's got a face drawn inside his catcher's mitt. Says it's his dad. But we don't go to the park much anymore. What's the use? It hurts too much to practice when I know I can't play. Anyway, Scott and I both got stuck with our dads, and our sisters got to stay with our moms. That sucks.

I'll go stay with my mom and Katie this summer, but it's not the same as having them living here—teasing them, joking around with them, always having stuff in the refrigerator, having my mom come talk with me at night when I'm in my room, avoiding old Gilbert. Summer's not enough.

I grab the leftover pizza from last night and zap it in the microwave, then pour myself a big glass of milk from the carton *I* bought on my way home from work last night. I thought parents were supposed to at least feed you 'til you turn eighteen. I guess Gilbert doesn't know that. Or if he does, he doesn't care.

I'm starving about now, but before I even get any food in my belly, my dad starts. "I talked to Mr. Grant from Loser High School today," he says.

"So?" Maybe that Merton teacher complained about what I wrote.

"So anytime you ain't there he's callin' me. And when that happens, that's the time I report your car stolen, so don't even think about cutting school," he says, sounding all tough.

I take a gigantic bite of pizza and start chewing, with my mouth wide open between munches, looking straight at him. He hates when I chew with my mouth open. I only do it in front of him.

I used to think he was such a tough guy, in his black uniform with his loaded gun. Not anymore though. I'm even bigger than he is now. He looks away. I can tell he's pissed, but I don't care. So am I. Just looking at him in front of the TV with his belly hanging out pisses me off. I'm glad I have to work tonight. As much as I don't love McDonald's, it's better than this place.

When I get to school in the morning, the principal, Mr. Dailey, and some of the other teachers are standing around the front gate, laughing and talking.

"Hey, Jason, how's it going?" he says.

"Okay," I say. I've never had a principal call me by name before, unless he had my records sitting in front of him and I was in trouble. This Dailey guy's just standing in the sun, shooting the shit. He doesn't even have a walkie-talkie. They must not put real principals at Sojourner High.

"Hey, Jason," Mr. Fowler says, walking over to me. "You used to play Little League?"

"Yeah."

"I thought you looked familiar when you came into class yesterday, but I couldn't place you," he says. "Pitcher, right? On Gary's Hardware?"

"Yeah."

"I coached the Flagg team the year you guys took the state championship. You still playing ball?"

"Nope. They wouldn't let me."

"Who wouldn't let you?"

"You know. The school. They said my grades weren't good enough."

"Oh. Too bad," he says. "Ever see Johnny, the kid who played third base on that team?"

"He moved to Bakersfield."

"He was a good ballplayer, too," Mr. Fowler says. "What about Scott, the catcher?"

"Yeah, he's on the team at Hamilton."

"You guys had an amazing team that year."

We did have an amazing team that year. It was the best year of my whole life. I was in seventh grade, doin' okay in school, had a girlfriend, Marci, who was totally in love with me. My family was still all together. But, best of all, Johnny and Scott and I were like the heroes of our team. I get this empty feeling in the pit of my stomach when I think of how things were then, and how they are now. If I could take a trip to anywhere in the universe, I would go back to seventh grade.

First period I sign in, get my folder, and sit down next to Mark in a beanbag chair. He opens his journal, which is in his folder, and starts writing. My journal is not in my folder. I take a magazine from the shelf behind me and start flipping through it.

Ms. Merton writes some stuff on the board. Thursday evening is a parent meeting, the Friday Nite Live group is going to Santa Monica for a clean-up-the-bay project—that kind of stuff.

Some girls are sitting at a table with nachos and Big Gulps, showing pictures like girls always do.

"He's sooooo fine," one of the girls says, practically drooling over a picture.

Ms. Merton walks over and stands by their table. "Time to get to work," she says.

"C'mon, Claudia," the almost drooler says.

"Nope. Put the pictures away. No credit for looking at pictures."

She stands there, and finally they all put their pictures into their backpacks and start writing in their journals. Ms. Merton walks back to her desk and calls me over. She motions for me to sit down. I see that she has my journal in her hand. Well, I don't care. I wrote from the heart, like she told me to do. It's a stupid school, anyway. Let her kick me out. What do I care?

"Nice job," she says. "This is well organized and to the point. You've expressed yourself well."

Is she being sarcastic, I wonder?

"Correct punctuation, correct spelling, very legible handwriting. Did you know you're a pretty good writer?"

I just stare at her dumbly.

"I'm not saying you're William Shakespeare, but you obviously can communicate clearly in writing."

I keep waiting for her to be mad about some of the words I used, but it doesn't happen. She hands me my notebook, tells me to do another journal writing for today, and she'll come over and talk to me about the reading part of the class.

"I know you say you hate reading, but maybe you just haven't found the right book yet."

"I hate reading," I tell her. Then I go back to my place beside Mark and try to figure out what to write about. A little later the teacher brings a book, *The Shining*, to Mark and hands it to him.

"Thanks," he says.

"The new one will be out in paperback next month," she says.

"I'll pick it up then."

"Cool," he says, handing her his journal and opening the book.

She hands me a couple of paperbacks. "Thin ones to start with," she smiles. "Just read the first page. If you don't like them, give them back."

One of them is *The Outsiders*. I've seen the movie and I remember the story. I could just pretend to read the book. I wonder if it's the same, or if it's one of those things where the movie is totally different, except for the title. I put both of the books on Merton's desk when I leave.

"Boring," I say.

Second period. I dread going into the Snake Pit. I'd leave now, but I sort of want to go to my third period computer class. Also I don't want old Gilbert calling his buddies at the police department and having them pick me up for auto theft. I doubt that Mr. Grant would call, though. They always say stuff like that and then they never follow through. At Hamilton High I once missed four weeks in a row before anyone called home.

I sit as far away from the snake, and the snake girl, as I can, writing in my physical science packet. Mr. Fowler brings a clipboard to the table where I'm sitting.

"Anyone here want to sign up for Saturday Work Day?" he says, putting the clipboard on the table. "Extra credit, make up days missed, plus you get the inner glow of knowing you're doing something nice for your school."

"More planters?" the guy sitting next to me says.

"Not this time. Tomorrow we're going to break up asphalt and plant three new trees."

The guy signs his name, then passes the clipboard over to me. I hand it back to the teacher. Then he turns to the whole class and asks, "Why did the turtle cross the road?"

Students groan. Mr. Fowler grins.

"To get to the other side," the snake girl says, sounding bored.

"No. That was the chicken," Fowler says. "I don't think you can pass life science if you can't tell the difference between a chicken and a turtle." Some of the kids laugh. Most don't seem to notice the conversation. He asks the question again, "Why did the turtle cross the road?"

"Just tell us and get it over with," the kid next to me says.

"Nobody knows? Jason?"

My face grows warm. I know it's turning red. I hate when teachers call on me.

"Nobody?" he says, pausing a moment, then telling us, "To get to the Shell station, of course."

Everybody groans.

"C'mon. You know my jokes are better than Pritchard's."

"Who's Pritchard?" I ask the guy next to me.

"He teaches history. They're always raggin' on each other about who tells the best jokes."

"Who does?" I ask.

"Neither one," he says, but he says it with a smile. "Teachers around here rag on each other all the time. Fowler and Pritchard are always saying stuff about how old Ms. Merton is—last week Pritchard went around to all the classes and invited them to a special assembly where Ms. Merton would be giving an eye witness account of some Civil War battle."

"What did she say?"

"Nothing. She laughed—they're a trip, man. One day they came to school all dressed alike, teachers, custodians, office ladies, everybody—white shirts, blue pants, blue headbands."

"Why?"

"They said they just wanted to see if anyone would notice."

This school is like a different planet compared to Hamilton. Teachers there take themselves very seriously. Come to think of it, except for Coach Hernandez, I don't think I ever saw a Hamilton teacher laugh.

At break time, Mark and I sit on a bench in the sun, eating nachos from the snack bar. I guess if I hang around long enough

I'll get used to it here. But, as my grandma used to say, that's a big if.

In the computer class Miss Keyes comes over and shows me what I can do for a special certificate. It looks like a lot of work.

"If you complete this, it can help you get a job working with computers," she tells me.

I'd rather just fool around with the computer than do a bunch of stuff for a certificate. She leaves a beginning worksheet for me and tells me to consider it.

"How're things going at Slowburner High School?" my dad asks one afternoon. What a wit.

"You heard from Mr. Grant?" I ask him.

"Nope."

"Well then, I guess they're going okay," I say.

"Hangin' out with the burn-outs and gang-bangers?"

"Yeah, Dad, whatever you say."

He's never happy. At least I'm going to school. I haven't missed a day in three weeks. That's a high school record for me.

"So what's this parent meeting I got a letter about?"

"What about it?"

"I ain't goin'."

"So?"

"So . . . I ain't goin'."

I don't know why he needs to tell me that. He's never been to a parent meeting in my whole life. My mom used to go, but he didn't. The only thing he ever went to was my baseball games, and that wasn't for me, it was for him. Big man in the bleachers could swell his chest and say that's my kid just made that play. I don't want him going there anyway. Wherever he goes now he talks about his bad luck, and how hard things are, trying to raise a family on disability. What a load of shit.

3

One day Merton brings a book over to me. It's about the twentieth book she's brought to me so far.

"Try this one," she says.

Another boring book, I think, but I start the first page anyway. By the time school is out for the summer I bet I will have read the first page of about a hundred books. Now even Mark is trying to find something for me to read—he keeps saying, try *Firestarter*, or *Carrie*, but I'd rather just see the movies. Anyway, this book starts out with a guy saying he's seventeen and he's already a loser. I can relate to that, so I go on to page two. I don't notice when kids get up to leave class until Mark calls to me from the door.

Merton takes the book from me. She smiles and says she'll hold it for tomorrow.

Halfway through third period, Fowler comes to the door and calls me out of class. I don't think I've done anything to get called out of class for.

"What's wrong?" I ask as I follow him outside.

"Nothing. I just want to talk to you about a way to earn extra credit and help some kids out at the same time."

I don't say anything. Everybody's always talking about extra credit around here—*opportunities* for extra credit. My idea of opportunities has to do with winning the lottery, not doing some stupid school assignment.

"Interested?" Fowler asks.

I shrug.

"You'd be good at it. The Lions Little League team lost their coach—he had a heart attack, so he's out of things for a while. They're in third place, a good little team, but they'll be knocked out if they can't find a coach to take over. You could get credit in Community Service and also maybe in Communications. How about it?"

"I don't know. I'm not sure how it would fit with my work schedule."

"McDonald's?"

"Yeah."

"The one over on Seventh Street?"

"Yeah."

"I can help you arrange that. I know your boss—he'll go out of his way for a good cause."

That's not what *I* think about my boss. From where I stand, it looks like he goes out of his way to give people a hard time.

"Think it over," Fowler asks.

"Okay," I say. But really, the only thing I want to do with baseball is play, not coach.

"Hey! Jason! Come out here!"

Even though I'm in my bedroom changing clothes, old Gilbert thinks nothing of yelling at me from the living room where he's sitting on his fat butt, like always.

"Just a sec," I say.

"I want to talk to you," he yells.

"Okay, okay," I say, walking out to the living room, still buttoning my Levis.

"That Grant guy called from your school today."

"I been going to school," I say, ready to be mad as hell if he's going to start in on me.

"I know," he says.

"So?"

"So he said he just called to say you're doin' good—told me parents are used to hearing bad news. He wanted to spread some good news."

"Yeah?"

I hadn't thought much about it, but I guess I *have* been doing okay. I've been there for six weeks now, no cuts, and I'm turning in work in all of my classes.

"He says your teachers are pleased with your progress." Then he starts laughing.

"What's funny?"

"You. It sounds like you're gettin' to be some kind of bigshot at Loser Tech."

Something snaps in me. I make a quick move so I'm standing over my dad and I look straight down at him.

"You know what?" I say, not waiting for an answer. "You're not such a winner. At least people at my school are trying to get their shit together. Looks to me like Loser Tech is right here in this living room . . ."

He's out of his chair faster than I've seen him move since he stopped wearing his uniform.

"Don't you call me a loser, you ungrateful bastard. Who do you think puts food on your table and a roof over your head?" he yells.

"The state of California," I yell back at him. We're eye to eye. His fists are clenched. So are mine.

"I earned this leave," he says, practically in a whisper. "Nobody needs to think I'm a loser, all I went through to maintain law and order—don't you ever, ever accuse me of bein' a loser."

"Yeah, well I don't like being called a loser, either," I say, backing away a little.

"I didn't say you, I said that school," he says, sitting back down in his La-Z-Boy recliner.

"My school, either," I say. "I've learned more there in six weeks than in the whole time I was at Hamilton."

"Like what?"

"Like how to use a computer, and that there are some books that aren't phony, and that snakes don't feel slimy, and that there are teachers who care."

He just looks at me, like he's looking at a stranger.

"I'll tell you something else," I say. "I've learned that school isn't so bad if there's not someone ridin' you all the time. I've got a say over what I do there. It's not everybody do the same thing at the same time just because teacher says. I won't say I like school, but I don't hate it now, and the people I go to school with aren't losers anymore than anywhere else."

I stand watching him, waiting for his next remark. He picks up the remote and starts channel surfing. I go back to my room to read until it's time to go to work. I'm reading the life story of Jim Morrison. It makes me laugh—he was so totally outrageous. But it also makes me want to cry. As outrageous as he was, and as stupid as he was to die so young, at least he was following his dreams. My dream of being a Dodger keeps getting farther and farther away.

The next morning the old hippie calls me into his office. He's got my school records spread out in front of him.

"I talked to your dad yesterday," he says.

"So I heard. He said he got a call from Loser High School."

Mr. Grant is quiet for a while. "Do you think you're a loser, Jason?"

"Like father, like son," I say.

"What's that mean?" he asks.

I shrug my shoulders.

"Listen, Jason. Lots of kids come here with the idea that they've already failed in life—that they're losers. The truth is, you're only a loser of you think you're a loser."

More of that school bullshit, I think.

He looks at me for a while, not saying anything. Then he

shows me this form that lists what I still need for graduation. It's a lot. I'm supposed to be a junior, but I've got the credits of a first semester sophomore.

"You screwed up," he says, like I need someone else to be telling me that. "That's the bad news. The good news is there's hope."

Here comes the full-of-shit, it's-up-to-you lecture. I stare out the window at a tree, counting leaves.

"I ran into Coach Hernandez at a meeting the other day. He asked about you. Said he wished you were still on the team—you like playing baseball?"

"Yeah."

"You know, if you could get caught up on credits, you could go back to Hamilton High in time for baseball second semester, play your senior year if you're still good enough."

I look at the form again. I'm 60 credits behind. Impossible.

"Interested?" Mr. Grant says. "If you're not, I'll not waste any more of your time or mine. If you are, I'll run down some possibilities for you."

"Go ahead," I say, interested, but without much hope.

By the time I leave Grant's office, I've got a plan in my pocket. It includes summer school, extra credit projects, information on how to get credit for working at McDonald's. It doesn't seem impossible. For the first time in a long time, I let myself think about playing baseball again.

First period I go over to the table where Merton is sitting. I sit down beside her. She gives me a funny look.

"Sometimes it makes me nervous when students sit next to me," she says. "But I guess *you're* okay."

I laugh. Really, I only sat next to her because I don't want anyone to hear what I'm saying.

"Could I get some homework? And another book to read?"

"Be still my heart," she says, clutching her chest.

I laugh again.

Second period I talk with Fowler about the extra credit

coaching thing. I can get ten elective credits doing that, so I say yes. For science he gives me a book and a series of questions to take home.

"Start here, on the page with the picture of Ms. Merton's first husband," he says, pointing to a picture of Cro-Magnon man. He doesn't crack a smile.

Period three I tell Miss Keyes that I want to work on completing one of those computer certificate things.

"Good choice," she says, and tells me what I need to do to get started.

I know it'll be hard to catch up, but right now, I think maybe I can do it. At Hamilton I tried to change lots of times. I'd tell myself that I would start going to all of my classes, pull my grades up so I could play ball. Then I'd get pissed off over something, a teacher nagging me about homework, or bugging me because I'd missed a lot of assignments, and I'd think to hell with it and stop going to class again. This time feels different though. I'm going to try to make it different. Really.

I call Scott when I get home and ask him if he'll meet me at the park and toss a few with me.

"Sounds good," he says.

Coaching Little League turns out to be a trip. The kids are mostly fifth graders. As soon as I walk on the field they start hanging on me, "Jason, Jason, can I play first?" "Can I play left field?" "Will you take me home after practice?" "Will you buy us pizza?" But they're a tough team, and they've moved into second place since I've been coaching them.

There's this one kid, Perry, who drove me nuts at first. He had about a zero batting average, and he couldn't hold on to the ball if someone walked up and handed it to him. I wished I didn't have to play him, but that's how it goes in Little League, everyone plays whether they're any good or not.

When Perry gets up to bat, everyone groans. I'm trying to get them to stop that, to say encouraging stuff, but inside, I groan, too. The thing that gets me, though, is this expression he gets on his face when he walks up to bat. It's kind of a smile and a frown combined, like maybe this time he's really going to hit the ball, get a home run, hear the cheers—and maybe not.

I've been taking extra time with Perry, before regular practice, to help him with keeping his eye on the ball and extending his arm when he throws. Simple stuff, but stuff he keeps forgetting. It's funny, I like the natural ballplayers. They remind me of Scott and Johnny and me when we were in Little League. But the kid that really grabs me is Perry.

In June I go see Mr. Grant for a credit check.

"Hey, Jason, how's it going?" he says, standing to shake my hand. I wonder, if it snowed would he still walk around in those sandals?

Mr. Grant gets out my records, calls my teachers to see how much credit I have in each class right now, adds a bunch of numbers, checks his addition, then tells me what I want to hear.

"You're doing great, Jason—making up credit at a good pace. Mr. Fowler says you're doing an excellent job coaching baseball. If you continue at this rate, you'll be qualified to go back to Hamilton High in September."

"September? Do I have to go back in September?"

"No. You can wait and return second semester if you want."

"And play baseball?"

"You'd be academically qualified to play, if you make the team."

I laughed. "I'll make the team."

"You know, this depends on the same kind of effort in summer school, too."

"I know."

"Sometimes students get tired, lose their motivation, fall back into old patterns—you getting tired? You must be busy all the time between school and work and coaching."

"I like it. I'm almost never home anymore, except to sleep."

"How're things with you and your dad?"

"Okay," I say. "He's still asleep when I leave for school in the

morning, and he's in bed when I get home from work late at night.
So we get along fine."

Summer school means I won't get to stay very long with my
mom and Katie in Tucson, but it's beginning to seem possible
that I'll have enough credit to go back to Hamilton second
semester of my senior year. Katie's going to come visit Dad and
me for two weeks, then I'll drive her back home when summer
school's over. She's twelve now. Mom says Katie's changed a
lot since I saw them last summer. God, I hope she doesn't have
boobs yet. I hate that, thinking of my little sister with boobs and
having a bunch of boys all horny over her.

The night before a game between the Lions and Vernon's
Pharmacy, I'm surprised to see Perry sitting on the back steps
when I get home from McDonald's.
    "What're you doing here? It's ten o'clock."
    He just sits with his head in his hands.
    "Come on, Perry. What's up?"
    "I'm quitting the team."
    "Just when you're starting to get good?"
    He keeps sitting there, not looking at me.
    "Do your mom and dad know you're here?"
    He shakes his head no.
    "Call them and tell them where you are. Then we'll talk."
    I walk him into the house and hand him the kitchen phone. My
dad is sound asleep in front of the TV. I turn it off, open a soda
for me and Perry, and sit at the kitchen table.
    "My mom wants to talk to you," Perry says.
    I take the phone and tell her I'll bring her boy home in a few
minutes.
    "Sit down," I say to Perry. "What's this about?"
    "Nobody likes me. I always strike out. I know I'll mess up in
the playoffs, and then everybody will hate me," he says, putting
his head down on the table, trying to hide his tears.
    "Perry, in the last game you got a hit that brought in a run,

and you helped make an out at third base."

"Yeah, but usually I just mess up. I'm a loser. Ask anybody and they'll tell you," he says, rubbing his eyes and his nose, still trying to hide the fact that he's crying. I take a paper napkin from the drawer next to me and hand it to him.

"Wipe your nose . . . Listen, Perry. This guy told me a while back you're only a loser if you think you're a loser. So I want you to stop with this loser stuff—it's not true and it messes you up."

"That's easy for you to say because you don't know what it's like to have everyone think you're a loser."

I laugh. "Someday I'll tell you my life story," I say. "Come on, I'll take you home. But you've got to promise to show up for the game tomorrow. Promise?"

Perry nods. "But it's hard."

"I know."

When I get back, my dad is sitting at the kitchen table looking over some papers. "That kid's got problems," he says.

"Everybody's got problems," I say. "Perry's better than he thinks he is."

"Maybe," my dad says, looking at me sort of like I'm a stranger to him.

I go to bed wondering how that "you're only a loser if you think you're a loser" load of shit came out of my mouth when I was talking to Perry. Maybe it isn't really a load of shit.

My dad surprises me one morning by being up and dressed when I get up for school.

"I made some coffee," he says. "Want some?"

"No, thanks," I say.

He's sitting at the kitchen table, his hands curled around a mug of coffee. He's freshly shaved, unlike most of the time I see him, and it looks like he's just had a haircut. He's wearing clean khaki pants and a sport shirt.

"Going someplace?" I ask.

"Yeah. Why?" he says.

"I don't think you got all cleaned up just to see me this morning," I say, opening the refrigerator to see if I can find anything edible. No luck.

"I'm gonna start a retraining program, for a desk job," he tells me. "I can't sit around like this no more. It's driving me crazier than ever."

"I thought they wouldn't *let* you work anymore," I say, remembering all the tests and meetings he had two years ago, after the "incident."

"Not on patrol. I can't take that pressure anymore. I know that and so do they. But I been talking to the association. They talked to the captain. Maybe it's gonna work out."

Suddenly he reminds me of Perry, the look he gets on his face when he gets up to bat. Like he's afraid to hope, but maybe, just maybe, something good is going to happen.

He looks down into his coffee cup. "Seeing you doin' better made me realize I should get up off my duff and make some changes, too."

I don't know what to say. I kind of want to pat him on the back or something. But I just stand there watching his Perry expression. For the first time in a long time it seems like maybe I could start liking my dad again.

Like I said in the beginning, since eighth grade my life's been getting worse and worse. But maybe things get better sometimes, too. I mean, between me getting back to baseball and my dad getting back to work, maybe things *can* get better. Not like I'm *counting* on anything, but I think it's possible—maybe.

Baby Help

Rudy has his faults. I'm not saying he's perfect.
But nobody's perfect. Right?

CHAPTER

1

In my Peer Counseling class today, we have a guest speaker from the Hamilton Heights Rape Hotline. I'm sitting in the back of the room, pretending to take notes, but really, I'm writing my name over and over again, as it is, and as it will be. *Melissa Anne Fisher, Melissa Anne Whitman, Mrs. Rudy Whitman.*

Melissa Fisher has thirteen letters in it. I think I've had a bad luck name. If my name changes to Melissa Whitman, with fourteen letters, maybe my luck will change. I think it will. I touch the bruise on my upper arm, lightly, through the sleeve of my long-sleeved blouse. Things will be different when my name changes.

Rudy and I have been together for three years now and, next to our baby, Cheyenne, he's the most important person in my whole life. And I'm important to him, too. Before Rudy and Cheyenne, I wasn't important to anyone but me, and that wasn't enough. Rudy has his faults. I'm not saying he's perfect. But nobody's perfect. Right?

At the front of the classroom the guest speaker is writing her name on the chalkboard. Paula Johnson. She says to call her Paula. She looks young enough to be a student here at Hamilton

High School, but Ms. Woods introduced her as a college graduate with a degree in social work.

"Let's define rape," Paula says, turning to face the class.

"Being forced to have sex when you don't want it," Leticia says.

"Right," Paula says. "How can someone force a person to have sex with them?"

"By overpowering them," Christy says.

"With a gun or a knife," Josh says.

Paula writes responses on the board, under types of force.

I write *Cheyenne Maria Fisher, Cheyenne Maria Whitman,* next to my own names, half listening to the talk about rape, half concentrating on the names in front of me. Cheyenne is two now. I love her most of all. Even more than Rudy. Even more than myself.

Last summer when we were practically dying of the heat, we went to Rudy's aunt's house, to use her pool. I asked Rudy to watch Cheyenne while I went in to the bathroom. I came back out just in time to see my baby fall into the deep end of the pool. I ran to that end, jumped in, grabbed her and held her over my head. I can't swim, but I didn't even think about that. I just knew I had to get her out. I was swallowing water, holding her up, when I felt her lifted from my hands. I sank down, my lungs burning for air. Rudy jumped in and dragged me to the side and his uncle pulled me out. I lay there coughing and gasping for air, sick with all the water I'd taken in.

Rudy said I was stupid, that he saw her, too, and could have rescued her faster. But I didn't care—all I saw was that she needed help. Anytime my baby needs help, I'll be there, even if it means risking my own life. That's how I know I love her more than myself.

"What if the girl asks for it?" Tony says.

"What do you mean?" Paula asks.

"You know—like if a girl is a big tease and she gets the guy all horny, and then she yells rape when he does what she's been asking for all along."

"So let's get this straight. The girl comes on to him, maybe she's wearing clothing that shows a lot of her body, and then he forces himself on her?"

"Well, yeah. But she asked for it."

"If any of you think that's okay, you've got a good chance of ending up in jail. Never is it okay, never is it legal, to force sex with anyone, young or old, male or female, friend or stranger. Never. She can take off all her clothes and strut her stuff right in front of you, but if she says no to sex, and you force yourself on her, you're committing rape."

Questions are flying around the room now. What if she says yes and you're already, like almost there, and then she says no? Can a girl ever rape a guy? What about if you've got these plans, like say after the prom is going to be the big night, and the guy rents a limo and takes her to a hotel and he's got condoms and everything because that's what they've planned, and then she changes her mind? What about if you're married?"

Paula writes the questions on the board as fast as she can. I write *Rudy Charles Whitman* on my paper. I write our names in a forward slant and a backward slant, dotting the "i"s with little hearts, getting my Flair pen out of my backpack and going over the ballpoint writing to darken it. I like how the names look, and how Whitman looks after Cheyenne Marie, and after Melissa Anne. I like the feel of the "W" under my pen. It's a prettier capital letter than the capital "F" of the name I've always had. I practice capital "W"s while the buzz of discussion goes on around me.

"Anytime anyone touches you in a way you don't like, that's abuse. It may be sexual abuse, or it may be physical abuse, but if you don't like it, and if you've made that known, and it continues, that's abuse."

"Are abuse and rape the same thing?" someone asks.

"Not necessarily, except in a general sense. They both bring great pain and suffering to another human being, the suffering continues long after the actual experience, and they are punishable under the law."

I hear the anger in Paula's voice and stop my writing to look up at her. I wonder if she's been raped or abused. I touch the sore spot on my cheek, fingering it gently so as not to rub off any of the cover-up make-up.

About five minutes before the bell is to ring, Ms. Woods gives us our assignment.

"Copy three of these questions from the board and write a paragraph about each of them. Don't worry about right or wrong answers. Write your opinions, and the reasons you think the way you do. Paula will be back tomorrow and we'll continue this discussion."

I turn to a fresh sheet of paper and write: *1. Is rape a sexual act, or an act of violence? 2. Is rape more likely to occur with a stranger or with someone the victim knows? 3. Is there such a thing as rape in marriage?*

I walk to my next class alone. Even though I'm a senior, I'm pretty new to Hamilton High. I've moved around a lot. My mom works for the race tracks, not with the horses or anything like that, but selling tickets to bettors and cashing tickets for the winners. She sells *a lot* more than she cashes in.

Anyway, most of my life I've not been in any one school for over three months. It's hard to keep friends that way, so I'm kind of a loner. My best friend since third grade was a guy, Sean Ybarra. His mom works for the tracks, too, so we always ended up at the same schools. He was a really good friend—someone I could talk to about anything. But Rudy freaks out if I even glance at another guy, much less talk to them. So I've kind of lost touch with Sean. The last time I talked to my mom, about six months ago, she said Sean was signed up to join the Conservation Corps. I'll probably never see him again.

Hamilton Heights is the longest I've lived in any one place. After Cheyenne was born, Rudy's mom said the baby and I could move in with them. My mom thought it would be a good idea, so

Cheyenne would know her father and all, and besides, she told me, it was hard enough for her to support herself and me, much less adding a baby to all of her financial responsibilities. She wasn't mean or anything, but I sort of got the idea she didn't want me and Cheyenne tagging along with her if there was someplace else we could go.

So, I've been living with Rudy and his mom, Irma, since Cheyenne was four months old. I don't think Irma was dying to have us move in with her, either. Rudy wanted us though, and with Irma it's pretty much what Rudy wants, Rudy gets. He's her youngest son. The two older boys live in Texas now, so Rudy's it. But Irma's okay. She's crazy about Cheyenne, so that's something.

Anyway, I've been at Hamilton High long enough to have friends. It's just that I'm so used to being a loner I don't know how to be anything else.

After school I get in the yellow Teen Moms van and ride to the Infant Care Center with Christy and Janine. I guess they're the closest to being my friends of anyone at school. We always talk about our babies. Janine's baby, Brittany, is two months older than Cheyenne, so I usually know what's coming next. Brittany started walking, and then two months later, Cheyenne started walking. Brittany started saying "no" to everything, and about two months later, Cheyenne started to say "no" to everything. They seem to be following a pattern. Except Cheyenne already says more words. Secretly, I think she's smarter than Brittany, but Janine thinks Brittany's some kind of genius. I guess that's how moms are. Some moms anyway. Maybe not my mom.

We get out of the van at the center and walk inside. This is my favorite time of day, when I watch Cheyenne, her blond curly hair falling over her face, playing on the floor, or sitting at the table with juice and graham crackers. She's got hair like mine, only mine's darker now than it was at her age. And she has blue eyes, the same as me. But she's built like Rudy, short and stocky.

I watch, loving her, and then the moment comes when she first sees me and her face brightens with her biggest smile. She runs to meet me, and I kneel down so she can reach her arms around my neck.

"Mommy, Mommy," she says, and I hug her and twirl her around. Brittany and Ethan come running to their moms, too.

"Cheyenne's had a runny nose today," Bergie (Ms. Bergstrom) says. "Be sure to check her temperature before you bring her out tomorrow."

"Okay," I say.

"Brittany, too," Bergie says, turning to Janine.

I give Bergie my homework packet. A requirement for having Cheyenne in the Infant Care Center while I go to school is that I have to be involved in a parenting class. The unit I'm working on now is Discipline for Toddlers. It helps me understand things better. Like how even little kids need to have some say over their own lives. I wish Rudy were taking the parenting class with me, because we disagree a lot. He thinks I spoil Cheyenne, and I think he says no just to be saying no. He plays with her though, and makes her laugh. I think my mom was right about Cheyenne needing to be around her dad, even if Mom was mainly saying that to get rid of us.

Cheyenne gets her backpack with diapers, a change of clothes, and empty bottles, and walks with me to the van. The other two moms carry their kids' backpacks, but Cheyenne always wants to carry her own. At the van, Cheyenne clutches her backpack with one hand and tries to get a grip on the first step with the other hand.

"Can I help you?" I say, reaching down to lift her into the van.

"No! Baby help!" she says, frowning at me. She manages to get one knee onto the lower step, reach the railing with her free hand, and pull herself up to the next step, still juggling the backpack. She walks determinedly down the aisle and climbs into her favorite seat, the next one up from the back.

"Baby help" was one of the first things Cheyenne learned to say. One day when she was only about a year old, I started to help her into her car seat. She started crying in frustration, saying, "Baby help. Baby help." At first I didn't understand what was wrong, or what she meant. Finally, I got it. I lifted her out of her seat, stood her on the driveway beside the car, and let her climb back in on her own. It's been "Baby help, baby help," ever since.

"I believe that is the most determined child I've ever seen," Bergie says with a smile. I know that's saying a lot, because Bergie's been in charge of the Infant Center for a long time, and she's known hundreds and hundreds of kids.

"I'm proud of her," I say. "You should see her fixing her cereal in the morning if you think getting in the van is determined."

"Well, good for her," Bergie says. "We all need to be determined in this world or we're lost."

I walk down the aisle and take my place beside Cheyenne. She already has her safety belt buckled.

"Mommy. Buckle," she says.

"Okay, Okay," I say, kissing her on top of her head.

"Buckle!"

I buckle my belt, wondering at how insistent she is that I buckle-up. I don't think either Ethan or Brittany notice any of that stuff.

2

Rudy's car isn't in the driveway when Cheyenne and I get out of the van. I'm glad. Maybe his boss finally gave him more hours. Rudy gets frustrated because we never have enough money. Like right now he wants new speakers for his car stereo but he can't afford the kind he wants. I get a welfare check once a month, but, except for a few dollars for clothes for the baby, that all goes to Irma to help with food and household expenses.

There's a note on the refrigerator from Irma, telling me to do the dishes from last night and to put away the clothes in the dryer—*her* dishes and *her* clothes. She works part time at Kinkos and she's always too tired to do anything else. I do *all* the housework and laundry. I don't care, but it seems like she could at least say please or thank you now and then. On the other hand, I guess it was nice of her just to take us in. I know she feels crowded sometimes. We all do. The house is two bedrooms, one bath, a tiny kitchen, and a small living room. The four of us, and our stuff, definitely fill up every inch of space.

"Juice, Mommy," Cheyenne says.

I pull her high chair up close to the counter where I can watch her, and give her a cup of apple juice. I fill the sink with hot sudsy water and wash Rudy's and Jerry's beer mugs from last night. I blow dishwater bubbles for Cheyenne and finish Irma's dinner dishes. Then I take the baby from her high chair, change her diaper, and wash her hands and face. After that, I gather up her toys and my books and take her into the living room where she can play while I do my homework.

It's nearly six o'clock when I hear the rattle of Rudy's loose and leaky muffler. I pick Cheyenne up and walk to the door to meet him.

"Hi, beautiful women," Rudy says, giving us each a peck on the cheek. I don't smell beer.

"Hey, Missy. Old Murphy wants me to work full-time on this new remodel job he just got. In two weeks, I should have some bad sounds in my car," he says, smiling, giving me the thumbs up sign.

"How about it, Baby," he says, taking Cheyenne from my arms and holding her high over his head. "You and Daddy'll go cruisin' and blast out the oldies, huh?"

Cheyenne smiles and a big glob of drool lands on Rudy's forehead.

"Thanks, Cheyenne," Rudy says sarcastically, handing her back to me. But he smiles. I think we're going to have a good evening.

"Maybe you should get your muffler fixed before you put money into new speakers," I say.

"Nah. That muffler will last for a while. I want something *I* want for a change."

"What about school, if you start working full time?" I ask.

"Ah, shit, Melissa. It's just that Independent Studies crap anyway. It doesn't mean anything."

"But it's a way to get a diploma," I say.

"I can learn more from Murphy . . . You and your diploma, anyway. You gonna be ashamed of me if I don't get that piece of paper?"

"No. It's just that, well, later on you might need it."

"Then I'll worry about that later on," he says. "What's for dinner?"

"I don't know. I haven't started it yet."

He gives me that look, like a cloud just settled on his face and a storm may be coming up. "How come you never have dinner ready for me when I get home?"

"I never know what time you'll be here."

"You could at least have stuff started."

"Yeah, well if I'd started anything last night it would have been burned to a crisp by the time you got home."

We could fight. I can feel it. I don't want to, but it might happen. We look each other in the eye, then I look away. Rudy reaches out and touches my cheek, on the spot with the cover-up make-up.

"Come on, Missy, let's go to Domenico's and get a big old pepperoni and cheese pizza."

"Pizza?" Cheyenne says.

We both laugh. The cloud has lifted.

I grab sweatshirts for me and the baby, and we walk together to the car. Rudy starts to lift Cheyenne into the car seat.

"Baby help! Baby help!" she says, pushing at him.

"Okay, okay," he says, and puts her down.

We stand and wait while she struggles to climb into the car, then into the car seat.

"At this rate, Domenico's will be closed by the time we get there," Rudy says, jiggling his keys. He's not as impressed with Cheyenne's determination as I am.

At the restaurant we take a corner booth at the side, away from everyone else. Cheyenne likes to hang over the back of the booth and check out whoever is there and whatever they're eating. Sometimes she likes to sing the ABC song for them. Some people think it's cute and some don't. The corner booth is safest for us.

Late that night, after Cheyenne is sound asleep in her crib and Rudy and I are stretched out in bed, he turns to me and puts his arms around me.

"Now that I'll be making more money, let's go to Vegas and get married," he whispers. "How about next month?"

Getting married is something we've talked about doing since before the baby was born, but for some reason we never get around to it.

"Things will be better when we're married because then I'll know you're mine for sure," Rudy says.

"Okay," I say, thinking of how Melissa Anne Whitman looked written out next to my Peer Counseling notes, how pretty the "W" was. "I'll be eighteen next month," I remind him.

"Let's do it on your birthday. That'd be a great birthday present, wouldn't it? And then I'd only have to worry about remembering one special day instead of two," he laughs.

"The 27th," I say.

"The 27th it is. I love you, Missy. I don't ever want to hurt you."

I feel tears welling in my eyes. I know he doesn't want to hurt me, it's just that he gets carried away sometimes, especially if he's been drinking.

Rudy is the first person in the world ever to really care about me. Even after three years he still gets worried if I'm not home right on time. And if he has to work on a Saturday, when I'm home from school, he calls me during his lunch time and break times, too, just to see what I'm doing.

I don't always like having to stay home all day just to answer his calls, but then I think how when I lived with my mom I could be gone for days before she'd even notice. Finally, with Rudy and Cheyenne, I'm important to somebody. I hold him close, feeling his heart beat against mine.

"Let's pretend to make another baby," he whispers.

"I'm on the pill, remember?" I whisper back.

"It's just pretend," he says, kissing me long and gentle, being the Rudy I love with all my heart, the Rudy I wish would never change. I slip my nightgown over my head as Rudy strips off his T-shirt and boxers.

"I love your skin against mine," I whisper.

Rudy groans softly, moving his hands to the places only he has ever touched. Quietly, quickly, intensely, we make love. After, when we're lying relaxed in each other's arms, I ask Rudy if he thinks there's such a thing as rape in marriage.

"God, you ask the strangest things," he says, groggy. "Where'd you come up with that idea, anyway?"

"We have this guest speaker in Peer Counseling this week. It's one of the questions I copied from the board for homework."

"No way," he says, in his sleepy voice. "One of the reasons a guy gets married is so he can have sex whenever he wants. How could that be rape?"

"But what if the wife doesn't want to?"

"It's part of the bargain," he says. "When you get married you belong to each other."

"I think it can be rape, even if the people are married," I say.

"That's your trouble. You think too much," he says. Then I hear his deep, steady breathing and know that he's asleep.

I walk into the Peer Counseling room and take a seat next to Leticia. Even though I'm a loner, Leticia and I talk sometimes. She's super friendly, and talkative, so I don't feel so shy with her.

"Which questions did you write about?" she asks.

I open my notebook and read them to her.

"Yeah, I chose that one about are you more likely to be raped by a stranger or an acquaintance. I thought stranger, but my mom thought acquaintance. I guess we'll find out today . . . What did you say for the one about being raped if you're married?"

"At first I thought no, because that's what my boyfriend thinks. But when I talked with the girls from Teen Moms this morning, they said yes, even if people are married it's still rape if a husband forces his wife to have sex against her will."

"So what did you put?"

"I put both answers, because I couldn't decide," I say.

Leticia laughs. "This is the only class on campus where you can get away with that. I doubt that old Horton takes two answers for a math problem—'Ah, the answer is x = 1,272. Or else it's x = 8,523.' Wouldn't he flip his cookies?"

It *is* a pretty funny idea. But in this class the actual answers aren't as important as showing that we've thought about the questions. I wish more of my classes were like Peer Counseling.

Ms. Woods checks attendance while Paula gets started discussing yesterday's questions. It's much more likely that a person will be raped, or murdered for that matter, by someone they know than by someone they don't know. And, she tells us, *anytime* a person is forced to have sex against their will, it's rape. Married or not. "And rape has very little to do with sex and a whole lot to do with violence," she says.

"Where I work at the Rape Hotline," Paula continues, "we've found that rape and other kinds of abuse often go together. Many rapists have been abused as children and also, for some reason, many children who have been abused are also raped some time in their lives . . . So, how do you define abuse?"

As in the discussion yesterday, everyone yells out answers while Paula races to write them on the board. Being hit, kicked, shoved, ridiculed, put down, made fun of, are some of the things students come up with.

"My dad is always putting me down, saying I'm lazy, I'll never amount to anything, stuff like that. Does that mean I'm an abused child?" Tony asks. "Can I sue my dad?"

"You can try," Paula says, "but you'd probably need plenty of money for lawyers if you take that approach."

Most of the students laugh, including Tony, but Paula goes on, all serious.

"I don't know how extreme your case is," she says to Tony. "But I do know that the chances are great that a few of you, maybe several, are right now living under abusive conditions—conditions that not only cause you great difficulty now, but will cause you difficulty for years to come. And some of that abuse is physical, and some is emotional, and it's all painful and damaging. And if you're in a situation where someone is telling you day after day that you're no good, that you're worthless, you are in an abusive situation and you need help with it."

The room is absolutely quiet now, as if no one is even breathing. I wonder if it's true that several of us are being abused. I wonder how many secrets are in this room?

"I think maybe the little boy who lives next door to me is being abused," Leticia says. "His mom yells at him all the time. He's really skinny, and he won't even talk to me, like he's afraid of me."

"I'm afraid of you, too," Josh says, and again there is laughter, and the mood lifts.

Paula passes out sheets with the names and numbers of hotlines to call if you suspect someone is being abused, or if you need help yourself. She talks about our responsibility to protect children who have no way of protecting themselves.

"I'm gonna call this hotline as soon as I get home," Leticia says. "Anonymous reporting. Right?"

"Some are anonymous and some you have to leave your name with."

"I'll start out anonymous," Leticia says.

We get a flier from a safe house for battered women. Besides their phone number there are two lists. "NO ONE DESERVES ABUSE" is the first one. It includes physical abuse, put downs, verbal abuse, having possessions damaged, interference with comings and goings, being harassed and spied on, being stalked, and being isolated. The second list is titled "YOU HAVE THE RIGHT TO" and it lists: Be treated with respect; be heard; say no; come and go as you please; have a support system; have friends and be social; have privacy and space of your own; maintain a separate identity.

I tuck the flier in my notebook and wonder about all I've heard today. I mean, I know hitting and kicking is abuse. Rudy doesn't do that very often, though. And the thing about having privacy and a space of my own, how does anyone have privacy with four people sharing a small two-bedroom house? The right to have friends and be social? I think about Sean, and the friendship I've lost.

On Wednesday Cheyenne has a fever so I stay home from school with her. Sometimes Irma helps out at times like these, but she had to be at work early this morning. It's impossible to do any schoolwork or housework with Cheyenne so fussy. I hold her and rock her and watch a talk show. It's about this famous hockey player who beat his wife to death. Well, he hasn't been convicted yet, but it's only obvious. They're comparing it to the O.J. Simpson case, where there was this history of abuse that kept getting a little worse and a little worse, until the wife ended up dead.

This psychologist is saying that for men who hit their wives, or their lovers, murder is a short step away. I turn off the TV and pour a small bottle of juice for Cheyenne. The doctor said the more liquids the better. She sucks at the bottle listlessly, her usually dancing eyes glazed with fever. God, it scares me when she's sick. I don't ever want her to be hurting, or in danger.

I hold her warm body close and rock her gently. I sing her favorite song to her, "The Circle of Life," from *The Lion King*. She has a tape of that music, and she plays it so often I've memorized the words.

She falls asleep in my arms, but I continue holding her and rocking her, watching her. In three more weeks Rudy and I are supposed to be going to Las Vegas to get married, but I'm not sure. I keep thinking about that abuse stuff. I've never thought about "abuse" or being "battered." I've just thought, Rudy got mad and lost his temper. But abuse, battered, those words sound so *extreme*. Of course, when he hits me it *feels* extreme.

3

The first time Rudy ever hit me was just a few months after we'd started being together. He's three years older than I am, so he was eighteen and I was fifteen. I think that time, when we first loved each other, was maybe the happiest time in my life. I was totally inexperienced with boys, not very pretty, and with my K-Mart wardrobe, I didn't expect to ever have a boyfriend. But Rudy saw me one day, standing in the rain, waiting for a bus. He offered me a ride. I never take rides with strangers, but I was so cold and wet, and he was so cute, I got in his car, and that was the beginning of it all.

But back to the first day he hit me. I was at the corner, waiting for the bus again, when Sean came running up to me. I hadn't seen him since Santa Anita closed its season the previous spring.

"Hey, Melissa," he said, "you look great. How've you been?"

"Good," I said with a smile, thinking of Rudy. "Really good. How about you?"

"Oh, you know, same old stuff. Listen, I've got to go for a job interview, but I really want to talk to you and get caught up. Here's my new phone number. Give me a call tonight, can you?"

"Sure," I said. "I want you to hear all about my boyfriend, and

I want to know everything you've been doing since I saw you last." It felt so good to be talking to Sean again.

We were just saying goodbye when Rudy came driving past. He made a big U-turn in the middle of the street and stopped in front of where we were talking. He reached over and pushed open the door and told me to get in.

"This is Sean," I said, starting to introduce them, but Rudy pulled me into the car and peeled away before I could even finish my sentence.

"What's wrong?" I said, thinking maybe there was some emergency or something, he was in such a hurry.

"What do you *think* is wrong?" he sneered.

"I don't know," I said.

"Don't act all innocent with me!"

He pulled the car to the curb, slamming on the brakes.

"What's wrong?" I yelled. "I don't know what's wrong."

He swung his right hand from the steering wheel to my face in an instant. He hit hard, with the back of his hand. I was stunned.

"Don't you ever let me see you talking to no guy on no street corner like you're nothing but a slut."

"That was Sean, my friend from a long time ago," I said, crying, holding my hand over my smarting cheek.

"Yeah, well, I'm your friend now. Not Sean, nobody else but me."

I was so hurt, my cheek, yes, but more, deep inside me. For the first time in my life I had felt loved and secure with Rudy, and in one quick blow he'd shattered those feelings.

"I'm taking you home," he'd said that day. "I've got to go to work, but you just stay at your house until I get there later tonight. You got it?"

I nodded.

"What did he give you?" he said.

"Nothing. We were just talking!"

"He gave you something. I saw him hand you something!"

"He just gave me his phone number," I said, taking the piece of paper from my pocket and waving it in front of him. He grabbed it from my hand, crumpled it, and threw it out the window.

"You wanna talk to someone on the phone, call me," he said. "Only me."

Once home, I washed my face and put ice on my cheek. When my mom came in from work and asked me what happened, I told her I'd tripped and fallen against a light pole. She just shrugged.

When Rudy came over that evening he asked if I would please go get a bite to eat with him. I had thought we were through, but when I saw the pleading look on his face I followed him to the car. We picked up a couple of burritos and drove back to his house.

"Come on in," he said. "My mom won't be around for a while."

He took a package from the glove compartment and we went inside.

"Sit by me," he said, patting the spot next to him on the couch. I hesitated.

"Come on, please, Melissa. Please, Missy."

I sat down and he pulled me to him. "God, Missy, you're the best thing that's ever happened to me. If you left me, my life wouldn't be worth shit."

He kissed my forehead, then nestled his head against my neck and shoulder. I could feel the warm dampness of his tears against my neck. I reached up and dried his cheeks with my hand.

"I'm sorry. I'm so sorry," he said. "It's just that I love you so much. I'm so afraid of losing you."

He handed me the box he'd taken from his glove compartment. In it was a gold bracelet with a single charm—a heart.

"This is to tell you I promise you, with all my heart, that I will never ever hit you again. I don't want to hurt you," he said.

I took the bracelet and he fastened the clasp for me. And I had hope again that someone loved me, that I belonged to someone.

In the past three years Rudy has hit me more times than I can count. I still wear the bracelet, but it doesn't mean much to me anymore. Usually he only hits me if he's been drinking, but lately he's been drinking more than ever. I think if he'd just stop drinking we'd be fine together.

Rudy's mom says I've just got to learn when to keep my mouth shut, like it's my fault when he hits me. I used to think that was right, but I'm beginning to think otherwise.

"He's like his father was," she told me once. "I finally learned how to handle him. I just shut up and stayed out of his way when he was drinking. That's all you have to do."

"Did you end up with a happy marriage?" I asked.

"I wouldn't say we were the picture of happiness, but at least he hardly ever beat the crap out of me after I learned to zip my lip. I guess we were happy enough. I sort of missed him when he died."

I don't know. Rudy says things will be better when we're married. He won't need to hit me anymore because he'll know I'm all his. But what if things aren't better when we get married? Then what? Sometimes, though, Rudy is really sweet to me. And I know he needs me. Not many people need me.

Cheyenne's bottle drops to the floor. I take her into our room and put her down in the crib. She stirs a bit, but she doesn't wake up. Maybe now I can get some reading done. I'm behind in English and history. Sometimes I have a hard time keeping up. Not that I'm stupid, but there's a lot to do, taking care of a baby and doing the housework and laundry for four people. Plus, I've got a lot on my mind.

When Cheyenne wakes in the morning she's bright-eyed again. She stands at her crib, smiles, and says "Up?" just like always. I am relieved to see her feeling better.

Rudy goes to lift her from the crib, but she starts saying, "Baby help! Baby help!" frowning and holding on to the crib slats. I go over and lower the side rail.

"Let her climb out by herself," I tell Rudy.

"Jesus Christ," he says, putting her down. "What's with this kid, anyway?"

"Nothing. She just wants to do it herself," I say.

"Well, everything takes twice as long with this baby-help crap."

"But she's learning how to do things," I say.

"So?"

"So, do you want coffee before you leave?" I ask, changing the subject.

On Friday, the last day that Paula is going to be in Peer Counseling, she brings the director of a battered women's shelter with her. This woman, Pam, tells us about the way they do things—how they protect women and their children from abusive husbands, how they help them find jobs and housing to get back on their feet. "It's a six-week program," she says.

I raise my hand and ask, "What happens after six weeks?"

Leticia looks at me funny, I guess because I never ask questions in class.

"After six weeks they get settled in another place—their own apartment, or a kind of half-way place, sort of a group center."

"How much does it cost?" I ask.

"No one is turned away because of money."

Pam says how hard it is for abused women to break away, and that some end up going back to their husbands or boyfriends.

"Man, I'd never do that," Leticia says. "That's *stupid* to the maximum!"

"Sometimes, in spite of reality, it's hard for women to give up on whatever dream they had of the man who's beating them. These guys can be very charming."

I look at my bracelet, the heart gleaming with sunlight from the window behind me. Charming is right.

A week before we're scheduled to go to Las Vegas, Rudy comes home late. I smell beer on his breath when he kisses me, but he seems to be in a good mood.

"C'mon, come listen to this."

I check on Cheyenne. She's sound asleep. I walk out to the car and sit in it. Rudy turns on the tape player. It's a rap tape that he knows I don't like, with the words over and over saying, "You're my bitch, my bitch, my bitch." He's got it cranked up so loud it hurts my ears. I get out of the car and walk back into the house.

"Hey, what's with you?" he says.

"I hate that tape, and besides, I think you should have bought a muffler. We're driving all the way to Las Vegas next week and your car sounds like it will barely make it around the corner."

Irma comes in and flashes me her shut-up look, but I don't care.

"Oh, you don't like my bitch tape, Bitch?" Rudy says, walking over to where I'm standing.

"No, I don't," I say, not backing away.

"Rudy, honey, why don't you come in the kitchen and I'll fix you a cup of coffee," Irma says. Rudy pays no attention.

"And you don't like how I spend my money, Bitch? The money I work my butt off for?"

"I didn't say that," I tell him. "I'm just worried about the car. I think it might not make it to Las Vegas."

"I told you. You think too much!" he yells.

"You can't tell me not to think, Rudy Whitman!"

"I can't? I can't?" he says. Then he does what I know he's going to do. He hits me. Hard. In the face. I fall backward against the couch. He hits me again, harder. I cover my face with my arms, sobbing.

"Rudy, stop," Irma is saying. "Stop now." She grabs his arm. He shakes her off and raises his fist again, then lowers it. He is red in the face, breathing hard. He spits at me, then goes to our bedroom, turns on the light, and starts rummaging through the drawer where he keeps the money he's been saving for our Las Vegas trip.

"Daddy?" Cheyenne says, waking.

I go into the bedroom, half-covering my face. I don't know how I look, but I'm sure it's nothing I want Cheyenne to see. "Up?" Cheyenne says.

Rudy walks over and picks her up.

"Baby help," she says, pounding her little fists against him. "Baby help," she says, starting to cry.

"Stop with that goddamned baby help crap!" he yells at her. He lifts her from the crib with a jerk. She's screaming now. I rush to her and pick her up. Irma runs into the room.

"I've had all I can take of this place—I think this and I think that, and this constant baby help crap! I'm outta here!" he says, taking the money from the drawer and walking out the door.

I hold Cheyenne close, rocking her back and forth. "It's okay, it's okay," I tell her over and over again, but she cries harder and harder.

"I'm telling you, Melissa, you'd better learn when to keep that mouth shut. You know better than to cross him when he's been drinking . . . Are you okay?"

"I don't know," I say.

"Is Cheyenne okay?"

"I don't think he hurt her physically if that's what you mean by okay," I say. I walk into the bathroom and start the water in the tub. I check my face in the mirror. It's already starting to swell. I take off Cheyenne's clothes and my own, and we get into the soothing warm water. I check out her legs and butt, stand her up, turn her around, have her lift first one leg, then the other, checking her over.

"It's okay, Baby, you're okay," I tell her. Slowly, as I wash her all over with the soft washcloth and soap, her sobs subside. But even after she stops crying, her little face looks tight and worried. I wash my own face now, very gently. Irma comes in with an ice pack.

"This will help the swelling," she says, then leaves.

After our bath I take Cheyenne back to her crib. I give her a bottle, to soothe her, and I crawl into bed, too. I don't think Rudy will be back tonight. Usually when he leaves like that he stays away for a day or so. I'm awake most of the night, tossing, turning, thinking. The left side of my face throbs. I refill the ice bag and take some aspirin and try to sleep.

In the morning, I am awakened by Cheyenne's voice calling, "Up?"

I go to the crib and lower the rail so she can climb out. She holds her arms out to me.

"Baby help?" I say to her.

She leans closer to me, frowning. "No baby help. No," she whispers.

I reach for Cheyenne and pick her up, then set her gently on the floor by the crib. I watch her as she stands quietly, as if she is unsure what to do next. I lift her back into the crib.

"Up?" she says, holding her arms out to me.

"Baby help?" I say, wanting so much to see her determined struggle to climb out of the crib by herself.

"No baby help. No," she says, reaching for me.

Again I lift her from the crib. In my head I hear Rudy's furious scream of "Stop with that goddamned baby help crap!" and suddenly the white hot anger I've not felt for myself starts in my belly and moves through my body, filling me from head to toe with a fiery rage, clearing my brain, showing me the way.

I'm getting out of here. I'm getting Cheyenne out of here. Maybe he could break my spirit. Maybe I didn't have much spirit to begin with. But he won't break Cheyenne. I shove as many clothes into her and my backpacks as I can. I change and feed her. Irma comes into the kitchen and asks how I am.

"Good," I say. "Really good."

She looks at me as if I'm crazy, but the truth is, for the first time in three years, I'm sane.

"You just be careful what you say when he gets home, and everything will be okay."

"I'll say what I want," I tell her. "I'll think what I want. And so will Cheyenne."

"You're asking for trouble," Irma says.

"I'm asking for a life," I say.

I wipe Cheyenne's face and take the tray off so she can climb from the high chair. She holds her arms out to me.

"Baby help?" I ask.

Still, she holds her arms up, waiting. I take her from the chair, get our backpacks and my notebook, and walk out the door. Halfway to the bus stop, Rudy drives up. He looks at my face.

"I'm sorry. God, I'm sorry," he says. "Get in the car. Let's go talk."

"I've got to get to school, Rudy," I say. "We'll talk tonight. Don't worry."

"You can't go to school with that face," he says. "What'll you tell people?"

"I'll make up a good story," I say. "I've got a lot of them."

"Jesus, Missy," he says, looking as if he'll cry. Then he looks at Cheyenne.

"Hi, Baby," he says. She hides her face in my shoulder. "Oh, God," he says.

"Go home, Rudy. Get some sleep. We'll talk this evening."

"Sure?"

"Sure," I say.

I don't feel sorry about making a promise I know I won't keep. I undo the latch on my gold bracelet and let it fall to the gutter.

At the Infant Center I ask to use the phone. I take the number from my Peer Counseling notebook and call. Six weeks. That's not long to try to figure out a new life for me and Cheyenne. But I've got to try. After I make the phone call, I explain to Bergie what I'm doing, and that someone from the shelter will come to get me and the baby around noon.

"You're doing absolutely the right thing," she says, giving me a long hug. "I've been worried about you. Light poles seemed to be getting in your way more and more often."

"I loved him so much," I say, feeling my throat tighten. "I thought we could make a life. I tried so hard."

Bergie pulls me to her and holds me while I cry, the way I've seen her hold the toddlers.

"He can be so nice. But then he can be so mean."

"Nice doesn't make up for what he's done to your face," she says, handing me a tissue. "You've got to go to a safe place, and

Cheyenne needs a safe place, too. Even if he never touches her, if she grows up seeing you pushed around, that's tremendously damaging."

"Will it be bad for her not to be with her father?"

"Not as bad as it would be to grow up around someone who beats on her mother."

Cheyenne, who has been sitting in a high chair eating graham crackers, calls to me, "Mommy. Up?"

I go over and take the tray off, waiting to see what she'll do. She just sits. I lean over to pick her up. She pushes me away.

"No. Baby help," she says softly, climbing down from the chair.

I smile with relief, a smile as big as it can stretch in my hurt face. "Baby help," I say.

What If?

Mostly, I want to be left alone. I want to sleep.
I don't want to think. I don't want to remember.

1

Foggy. Gray. Where am I? I try to open my eyes. From far away, a voice breaks through.

"Did you see that? His eyelids fluttered! I saw it. Didn't you see it?"

"Are you sure?"

"Paul, Paulie, we're here. Don't give up. Oh, don't give up."

The voice is closer now. It's my mother. She's crying. Why? I try to talk but my mouth won't open. I feel her warm, wet cheek against the back of my hand.

"Mom," I say in my head, but I'm pretty sure the word doesn't come out.

I hear my grandma's voice. "Go home, Sylvia. Rest for a while."

"I saw it!" she says.

What's going on here? I try again to open my eyes, but it's as if they're sealed tight.

"Paul? We're here, M'ijo," my grandma's voice comes to me.

"You saw it, too, that time, didn't you? I'm not imagining it?" my mom says.

"Por el amor de Dios," Grandma whispers.

Other voices now, talk of fluttering eyelids. I want to hear more, stay longer, but the fog is back, gray and heavy in my head.

Something warm, damp, dabbing at my face and around my lips. A gruff, melodic voice says, "Oooh, boy, you gonna wake up with one mean headache. *If* you wake up. I think you gonna, though."

The sound of a washcloth being rinsed, then the warm dampness across my arm.

"You bad, but you not done. That's what I think."

"What?" I try to say. The washing stops.

"I felt somethin' just then. I bet you comin' out soon."

Fading. I fight to listen, to feel the wet cloth against my skin, to stay, but the fog creeps over me, pushing me under.

My mother's voice. I try to turn toward her. Nothing moves.

"Where am I?" I ask.

"Paul! I'm here. It's okay, it's okay," she says, in the soft tone she always used when I was younger and awakened by a nightmare.

Another voice. "You rang for a nurse?"

"Yes. He just tried to say something. I'm sure of it."

Cool hands touch my wrist. Taking my pulse?

"What did he say?" the unfamiliar voice asks.

"It was a mumble. But I know he tried to talk!"

Light. Ceiling. My mother's face hovering over me.

"Look! His eyes are open!" she says, and now another face next to hers, looking down.

"Can you hear me, Paul?" the person who is not my mother asks.

"Yes," I say, but know it comes out in a whisper.

She shines a tiny light, first in one eye, then the other. "You've been in an accident. You had a head injury. You can't turn your head or lift up because we have you in a special frame to keep you immobilized. It's temporary."

"What accident?" I try to ask, but the words are stuck again.

I feel the light pressure of my mother's head against my upper arm, nuzzling. What accident, I wonder, as the fog overwhelms me.

The ceiling shines white above. Hospital smells surround me. My mom and grandma are sitting side by side, next to my bed, looking intently at me.

"You're going to be all right now, Paul. I know it," my mom says. Tears are running down her cheeks. My grandma is clutching her rosary and smiling at me the way she did when I first learned to tie my shoes.

A man's voice. Someone I don't know. "How are you doing, Paul?" He's wearing a white jacket over regular clothes and he's got one of those stethoscope things around his neck.

"Do you know where you are?"

"Hospital," I manage to croak out.

"Good. Tell me your name."

"Paul Valdez."

"I'm Dr. Baines," he says. "Your neurologist. Can you tell me your address?"

"2120 South Bridge Street, Hamilton Heights."

"I didn't quite catch that. Can you speak a little louder?"

I try again, forcing more sound up my throat, through my mouth.

"Good," he says, writing something on a clipboard. "How old are you?"

"Seventeen . . . I'm thirsty."

"Which is it—seventeen or thirty?"

"No. *Thirsty*," I say, trying to speak clearly.

"Mary, would you help Paul drink a little water?"

Another unfamiliar person. A dark, friendly face.

"Little sips," she says, as I feel a straw at the edge of my mouth. I try to reach for it, but my arms are stuck on something. I suck gently at the straw. My mouth feels funny, like my lips are big as a camel's. I take another sip and she pulls the straw away. "Only a little," she says.

"What happened?" I ask.

"An accident. Can you wiggle your toes?" the doctor asks, pulling the sheet back.

I wiggle my toes.

"Good."

"Why can't I move my arms?" I ask, scared. There's so much I don't know.

"Try," he says, watching me carefully. I try, but they don't seem to go anywhere.

"You've got movement," he tells me. "We've got you pretty much immobilized for now, until your head heals. You're in what we call a halo. Do you feel like an angel?" He smiles at me. I don't know what the hell he's talking about.

"What's wrong with my head?" I try to ask, but I'm too tired to get the words out, and then I'm pulled back into the foggy place.

"Good signs here," the doctor says as I drift away.

"Come on. Take a sip of broth. Start gettin' strong again."

I feel the straw, sip, and get a taste of something warm. I force my eyes open.

"I knew you was in there," she says. "Didn't I say he was in there?"

"We knew, didn't we, Mary?" My mother answers, smiling down at me. I try to smile back, but my lips are big and stiff.

"Are you in pain, M'ijo?" she asks.

I think about that, think about my immobilized body. "My legs," I say. "My back."

"You're all bruised up, but nothing's broken," she says. "We've been so worried about this head injury, but the doctor thinks you'll be fine, given a little time."

"But what happened?"

"It was a drunk driver," she says, her voice filled with bitterness.

"But where? When?"

"You've been unconscious since Friday night," she says.

"Today's Wednesday. We thought we might lose you." She chokes back tears.

"But . . ."

"Don't worry about anything, Paul. Just rest and get well. It's okay," she says, rubbing my arm.

I move my feet. But how do I *know* they're moving? I can't move my head to see anything but the ceiling and a glimpse of people sitting next to my bed or standing over me.

I've heard of people who feel like they're moving their legs even after they've been amputated. What if it just feels like they're moving and nothing's happening? God! My heart pounds at the thought.

"Watch my feet, Mom," I say.

"You're moving your feet and your legs, Honey."

"Sure?"

"Positive," she says. Then she gets a little mirror from her purse and holds it in a way that I can see my feet move.

I wake with a start. I am trying hard to figure something out. Now my grandma is in the chair where my mom was before. She smiles. "Dr. Baines says you're gonna get well."

Something is trying to get up through the murk and fog. What is it?

"GABRIEL!" I yell, trying to rise from the bed.

"Shhh. Don't worry," my grandma says.

"Where's Gabe? . . . Abuela?" She doesn't look at me. I close my eyes and try to remember.

Unconscious since Friday. What was Friday? Don't know. Thursday? Track meet. I remember that. I ran second in the 800 meter. Gabe took first in the 100 meter. We won the relay, so Hamilton High did okay.

The week before, when Gabe and Eric were both out with the flu, we sucked. But Thursday was good.

God. Everything hurts. My mouth feels like it's filled with cotton. I'm so tired. What was after Thursday?

I am jarred awake by a nurse, a guy, who takes my blood pressure, temperature, pulse, and checks my eyes with one of those little flashlight things. "You had a close call," he says.

"Where's Gabe?" I ask.

"Who?"

"Gabe. My friend who was with me."

"Oh. I don't know. I just got back from vacation yesterday."

I remember that I had a test in Spanish on Friday morning. I hate that class. I thought it would be easy, because I already knew some Spanish from my grandma, and from Gabe's family. I didn't know I'd have to take tests on a lot of grammar stuff.

Then what? Oh, yeah, I went to Gabe's house after track practice to help set up for his grandfather's eightieth birthday. Gabe's family is like my family, and the other way around, too. Since I was three it's been just me and my mom and grandma. I always wanted a bigger family, and I got it when we moved in next door to the Sandovals, back when I was nine. There are five kids, a mom and dad and a grandma and grampa over there. The two oldest kids live somewhere else now, but it's still a lot more lively at Gabe's house than it is at mine.

Anyway, Gabe and I cleaned up the backyard—mowed the lawn and trimmed back some low branches that people could run into if they weren't careful. We took his mom to the liquor store to pick up the keg. The three of us crammed into Gabe's little Toyota truck.

"Better ease up on the tamales, Jefita," Gabe said to his mom.

"Big is beautiful, M'ijo, and don't you forget it," she laughed, scooting her butt back and forth, crowding us both.

Gabe's always teasing his mom about being fat, but I notice he's never chosen a thin girlfriend. And believe me, Gabe has his choice. Girls are always hanging around him, playing up to him. Not me. They hardly notice I'm there.

Were we in Gabe's Toyota, I wonder. Who was driving?

My head hurts. I need water. How bad off am I really? What if I can't walk? God, don't let that be.

My mom is sitting by the bed, reading. My grandma is next to her, crocheting. When Mom notices I'm awake she puts down her book. "The doctor says they can take you out of the brace later today. The swelling in your brain has gone down."

"Was Gabe hurt?" I ask. Grandma nods her head yes and looks back down at her crocheting.

"Is he in this hospital?"

"No, he's somewhere else," my mom says.

"How bad is he hurt?" I ask.

"Listen, Honey, don't worry about Gabe right now. Just concentrate on getting yourself well."

My grandma looks up and sighs, "Sylvia . . ."

"Not yet," my mom hisses.

And then I know. I don't remember, but I know. Gabe is dead. I let the fog come back in. I don't fight it. Maybe, when I wake up, we'll be at the birthday party in Gabe's backyard, with the smell of meat cooking on the grill and the laughter of all the aunts and uncles and cousins filling the night, and Gabe and me horsing around with the others. Like always.

Dr. Baines is standing over me, fiddling with the contraption that's been holding my head still.

"Your CT scan looks good," he says, loosening something and jiggling the "halo." Pain shoots from the front of my head to the back of my neck. Bright light jumps around behind my eyes. Damn!

"It's okay," he says. "The slightest movement will be a jolt at first. We can kick up the intravenous pain medication if it gets to be too much for you."

He eases the brace off and the sharp pains turn to dull aches. Very carefully, I turn my head toward my mom who is standing on the opposite side of my bed. For the first time I notice all the flowers and balloons crowded into my room.

"We'll be getting you on your feet later this evening," the doctor says.

"No two milers yet, though," Mom says.

"You a runner?" Dr. Baines asks.

"800 meters, 330 low hurdles, distance events, you should see this guy in action," Mom says.

Thoughts float through my aching head—me and Gabe practicing passing the baton for relay events, the wind against my face and the pounding of my feet against the track, the burst of strength that comes just when you think you can't go any farther.

"I used to run track in school," the doctor says. "Now the best I can do is a 5-K a couple of times a year."

Why are they talking about track? Sooner or later I'm going to hear what I'm trying not to think. Gabe's dead. Who was driving?

"You've got tons of get well notes here," Mom says, holding a stack of cards in her hand. "Shall I read them to you?"

"Sure," I say. What does it matter? Read the cards, don't read the cards. Gabe's dead.

By Friday morning I am free of tubes and monitors and able to walk to the bathroom by myself. My mom and grandma come in just after I've had breakfast. My mom works at Nordstrom's, in their credit office, and my grandma works in the kitchen at a convalescent hospital near our house. I guess they've missed a lot of work lately.

"The doctor says you should be out of here in another couple of days," Mom says, smiling.

"I'm ready," I say. It's still a little hard to talk. My mouth is all swollen and three of my teeth are loose. I hope I can keep them.

I'm sitting up in the raised hospital bed, propped up against pillows, watching TV. I feel like shit. Mom turns the TV off and she and Grandma each sit next to my bed, looking very serious. My mom takes my hand. "About Gabe . . ." she starts.

"I know," I say, hoping I don't have to hear the words.

"Are you getting more of your memory back?"

"No. I just know he's dead. You would have told me if he was okay. I know from what you're not telling me."

"You couldn't help it," Grandma says.

"Who was driving?" I ask.

"You were," Mom says. "But the other guy was so drunk, he went speeding right through a red light. There were plenty of witnesses. He's in jail now. It was his third drunk driving offense. He didn't even have a license."

"What car were we in?"

"Yours," Mom says. "And a good thing. If you'd been in Gabe's little truck, you'd both have been killed." She pauses, choking back tears. My grandma sits, head down, not looking at either of us. After a while, Mom continues. "The Dodge is totaled, but it wasn't fully crushed . . . It's a good thing you were wearing your seatbelt."

"Gabriel was thrown out of the car," Grandma says, still looking down.

Mom says, "I know you don't remember the accident, and I hope you never will, but believe me when I tell you there was absolutely nothing you could have done to avoid being hit by that drunk."

"Gabe wasn't wearing a seat-belt?" I ask.

"No," Mom sighs.

"You sure?"

"I'm sure."

"I'm really tired," I say.

"We'll be back this evening," Mom says. "I'm going to spend a few hours at work today. Call me there if you want." She pauses, looking at me. "Do you remember my number there?"

"Yes," I say, but when I try to think of it I draw a big blank. She leaves the number for me on a piece of paper beside the phone. I slide down in the bed, turn on my side, and will myself to sleep.

"Time for you bath," Mary says.

I turn over and open my eyes. She is beaming down at me.

"Can't I just take a shower?" I ask.

"No, Baby, you still too shaky-shaky."

I lie still while she washes me all over. I like Mary, but there are some things a guy would rather do for himself.

In the late afternoon Mr. and Mrs. Sandoval come into my room and pull chairs up next to my bed. They sit close to each other, holding hands. With her free hand Mrs. Sandoval reaches for mine.

"I'm so glad you're better, M'ijo," she says, her eyes filling with tears. "For a while, it looked like we'd lost you both." Mr. Sandoval, always the quiet one, glances around at the flowers and balloons.

"Where were we?"

She looks at me, blankly.

"The accident," I say.

"Corner of Fourth and Sycamore," Mr. Sandoval says, looking directly at me for the first time since he sat down. "You boys didn't have a chance. My strong, happy boy died because somebody had too much to drink."

We are all three silent, not looking at one another for a long time. Then Mrs. Sandoval says, "He didn't die for nothing."

"What do you mean?" I ask.

"His heart, his lungs, his liver, they're all helping someone else who needs them," she says, crying openly now, gripping my hand so hard it hurts. I don't pull away though. She can crush my hand to pieces for all I care. "Part of Gabriel is going on," she says.

I'm trying to understand. They've cut Gabriel up and given pieces of him away? I mean, I know that sort of thing is done, but Gabriel?

"He would have wanted it," Mr. Sandoval says.

"We just came to tell you that, Paulie," Mrs. Sandoval says, calling me by my little boy nickname. "We wanted you to know Gabriel didn't die for nothing."

I feel my chest swelling with sorrow and I fight back tears. My mom walks into the room and the Sandovals stand up.

"Don't go, Dolores," Mom says, but Mrs. Sandoval tells her

they only planned to stay a few minutes anyway. The two moms hug each other. Mrs. Sandoval bends over and kisses me on the forehead, and then she and Mr. Sandoval leave.

"My heart goes out to them," my mom says. I think how Gabe's heart has *really* gone out to someone. I close my eyes and wait for the fog to come.

2

The first week I'm home, practically everyone I know drops by my house. Eric and the guys Gabriel and I usually ran relay with come over after a track meet to cheer me up.

They tell me the details of the meet: Eric took first in the 200 meter. Hamilton didn't place in the 100 meter. That was Gabe's specialty.

"We'd have won the relay, too, except Tyler dropped the goods on the pass."

Tyler groans.

"As soon as you get back, you've got to practice handing off the baton with Tyler. Remember how Gabe used to always drop it until you guys practiced together a billion times?" Eric says.

We laugh, remembering our frustration with Gabe. "I'm fast," he'd say. "I use my feet, not my hands." But once he got good at passing and receiving the baton, we almost never lost a relay.

"Remember how he'd smile that 'eat my dust' smile when he was running?" Eric says.

"Yeah," Tyler says, "and Coach would tell him people can't run and smile at the same time. And Gabe would say he couldn't help it."

It's like, for a minute, Gabe is back with us, and then the conversation stops and there doesn't seem to be anything else to say.

"They oughta kill that drunk son of a bitch that ran into you guys," Tyler says.

"A guy like that doesn't deserve to live," John says.

Everybody nods in agreement. Then, after a long, awkward silence, Eric asks me, "When can you come back to school?"

"I don't know. Next week I'll get started with a home teacher."

"Cool," Manny says. "I'd like that a lot better than school. Kick back at home, watch a little TV, and once each day have school brought to your door."

"That's stupid," Ken says. "You'd be so bored—no girls, no track."

"Girls could come to my house like the home teacher," Manny says.

I try to stay with the conversation, say something now and then, but it's meaningless to me.

My ex-girlfriend, Desiree, stops by with flowers and a card that's signed "love." Two weeks ago I would have been all excited about that. It doesn't do much for me today.

I still hurt all over, and if I turn my head fast, or get up out of bed quickly, it feels like thousands of sharp needles poking inside my skull. Mostly, I want to be left alone. I want to sleep. I don't want to think. I don't want to remember.

My mom and grandma think I should never be alone in the house. Mom says, "What if something would happen when we're both gone?" I hate to tell you, Mom, I think, but something has *already* happened.

Anyway, my grandma has switched to the night shift at the convalescent home so she can be home with me all day, until my mom gets home from work. My grandma's answer to everything is to make menúdo. I *hate* menúdo, but she wants me to eat it every day.

"Can't I just have canned chicken noodle, Abuelita?" I whine, wondering why I'm acting like a six-year-old but doing it anyway.

"Menúdo will make you strong," she says.

The good news is I can walk to the bathroom on my own now, so I can dump my menúdo down the toilet when my Grandma leaves the room. The bad news is I stay hungry until dinner time.

Gabe's fourteen-year-old sister comes over on Saturday with a bunch of pictures to show me.

"Here's one at the carwash," she says. "Kids from the track team made over four hundred dollars to help with expenses. That was so nice."

Sometimes Monique looks like she's still ten, and sometimes she looks like she's about twenty. Right now she looks ten.

"Here's one outside the church, before the funeral. There were so many people—there wasn't even room for everyone inside. I'm sorry you couldn't be there."

"Why?"

She looks shocked. "Because you were Gabe's best friend. Because it was our last good-bye."

"I've never been to a funeral," I say.

"Mom says we were sending Gabe's soul to God . . . Look, this is at the cemetery," she says, pointing to a fresh mound of dirt. "He's next to my tía, so he won't be lonely."

Lonely?

"When you're better we can go visit him together," she says.

Nothing is making sense to me. "Monique," I say, "I'm so tired. I've got to go back to bed for a while."

I walk out of the den where we've been sitting and down the hall to the bedroom. I pause at my dresser and pick up the baton Gabe and I used to practice with. It's sticky with old sweat, mine and Gabe's. I set it back down and ease into bed. It's cool and dark in my room—like where Gabe is, surrounded by cool and dark. I wait for the fog.

Hector, Gabe's older brother, comes over Sunday morning. "Looks like you're getting around better," he says as he watches me walk into the kitchen and get a soda for him. We talk for a while, about the engine he's rebuilding in his garage, about the Lakers, about nothing. Then he says, "Mom wants me to remind you to come for dinner Wednesday night."

How can I do that, I wonder. Back when I was ten years old, I started eating dinner at Gabe's house on Wednesday nights because my mom had an evening class and my grandma was working an evening shift. And then it became a habit. I liked the bustle of the big family, everyone talking at once around the table, the shifts between Spanish and English, the fights and the laughter. I loved my mom and my grandma, but things were very dull at our house in comparison to the Sandovals. But I don't think I want to sit at that table and not see Gabe between his dad and Monique, teasing his mom about too many tamales on her thighs.

"I don't know if I'm ready to do that or not," I tell Hector.

He looks me in the eye in a challenging sort of way. "I think it would be good for my mom," he says.

How many lives have changed with that one accident? I don't want to count.

Ms. Woods, my Peer Counseling teacher, comes to see me Monday afternoon. I really like Woodsy. Everybody does. But I'd rather not see her today.

"I hear you're depressed," she says.

"I guess."

"It's not your fault," she says, just like everyone else keeps saying.

"How do you know?" I ask.

"Paul, stop torturing yourself. You were broadsided by a drunk driver who went through a red light traveling sixty miles an hour. You and Gabe were just in the wrong place at the wrong time."

"'Specially Gabe," I say.

"I worry about you, Paul," Woodsy says.

"Don't," I say.

After she leaves, I take another codeine tablet and go back to my bedroom. I try for sleep, but instead I lie staring at the ceiling, pushing thoughts out of my head, longing for the fog that came so often in the hospital but not often enough now.

Distant traffic sounds, birds chirping outside my window, my grandma's Spanish soap opera, Hector whistling in his garage as he tinkers with the engine, the codeine—then sleep.

Bam! I am startled awake by the loud clash of metal on cement. Hector yells, "Oh, shit!"

Only it's not Hector I hear in my mind, it's Gabe. And it's not Hector's engine hitting the garage floor, it's the clash of metals as the car from nowhere rams into us, spinning, spinning, rolling, rolling, everything yanked, jarred, crushed. Something presses hard against my head. I struggle to get free. Reach for Gabe beside me and find only space. Sirens, flashing lights, and then the fog.

I try not to think of it, but it comes again. Gabe's voice, screaming, "Oh, shit!" and the replay. And then it comes to me, the whole night. The night I don't want to remember. The details that scare me to think about.

It was el abuelo Sandoval's birthday party. Gabe and I were sitting out back watching his cousin do card tricks for Monique and some of the younger kids. It was around ten, but still warm out.

The small white lights we'd strung up earlier made everything look prettier than it ever looked in the daytime. I was on about my third plate of ribs. No one cooks ribs like Mr. Sandoval does. Gabe and I each had a beer while we were working in the yard before the party, and I had one with my ribs. Maybe two. No big deal.

"Hey, Paul," Hector yelled at me. "Mom wants me to go get more ice cream and your car's in the way."

"How come you always park in *my* driveway?" I yelled back.

"'Cause my driveway's always full," he laughed.

"I'll move my car," I said, putting my plate down and reaching into my pocket for the keys.

"While you're in the car, you might as well drive on up to the store and get the ice cream—two gallons of vanilla," he said, walking over to me and handing me a ten dollar bill. "And she wants the change. That's why I'm giving it to you and not to my brother," he laughed.

"C'mon," I said to Gabe.

We got in my car with Monique tagging along behind. "I want to go with you," she said.

"Nah," I said. "We'll be right back." I drove off, leaving her standing in the driveway.

"She's in love with you, you know," Gabe told me with a laugh. "She carries a picture of you in her wallet."

"At least someone does," I said. "But I'm no cradle robber. Besides, she's like my sister."

"She'll get over you," Gabe said. "Everybody else does," he laughed.

"Hey, that's cold," I said, laughing along with him. I don't have a reputation for being lucky in love.

"Do you want to go with me to Angie's after awhile? She's got a friend staying with her tonight," he said.

Ever since Desiree and I broke up, Gabe was always trying to set me up with someone.

"Is her friend twelve years old, like the last one?" I ask.

"So, now and then I make a mistake," he said with a laugh. Then—"Oh shit!" and next—crash, spin, roll, sirens, lights, fog.

It'd been kind of a game with Gabe. He'd get in my car and sit there, waiting for me to start. "Buckle up," I'd say.

"Lighten up," he'd say back.

We'd sit and joke around, and then finally he'd buckle up and we'd take off. That's how we were even from a long time ago. I was more cautious and he was freer. That's why he was a sprinter. He liked the thrill of top speed, not having to pace himself, just running full out. Me, I like a long race, where I have more control, where I can run with a strategy.

"Don't be so serious," he'd tell me. "Take it as it comes."

"Like the baton?" I'd say sarcastically, reminding him of how many times he dropped it and lost relays for us until he got serious about learning the pass.

I used to wish I could be more light-hearted, like Gabe. So it surprised me when he told me that he wished he was more of a planner, like me. Maybe that's why we were such good friends. We each supplied something the other person was missing.

Anyway, it was like my job to make him wear his seat-belt, and it was his job to make a big joke out of it. But I was serious about the seat-belt thing because once, just before I got my driver's license, we saw this really gory film in health and safety. It showed all of these terrible accidents in which people had died or been messed up for life. And it showed crash tests with dummies with seat-belts and without seat-belts, and the seat-belts made a huge difference. Right then I decided I'd always wear a seat-belt and anyone riding with me would, too. I never, before the night of the accident, took Gabe anywhere if he wasn't buckled up.

Here's the thing, though. The worst thing of all that I try never to think about. Was it because I'd had two beers, maybe three, that I forgot to make him buckle up—that I forgot our game? Would he be alive today if he'd been wearing a seat-belt to keep him in the car instead of flying out onto the street?

I don't care how many times I hear "It wasn't your fault—it was a drunk driver," I'll always wonder if there was more than one drinking driver that killed my friend. What if I'm as much to blame as the guy who ran the red light? The guy who's in jail for what he did?

3

"**D**olores Sandoval called last night, after you were in bed," Mom says, standing in the doorway of my bedroom, buttoning her coat, ready to leave for work. "She said they missed you last Wednesday night at dinnertime and hope they'll see you tonight."

I turn over, facing away from my mom.

"Paul, I think you're well enough to go over there now, aren't you?"

"I still get really tired," I say.

"Well, the doctor says you should be doing more now. Did you go for a walk yesterday, like he told you?"

"No. I just didn't feel like it."

"Try it today, will you?" she says.

"Yeah," I say, but I'm not sure I mean it.

"Is there anything you want me to bring home from the market?"

"No."

She stands quietly in the doorway for a while, looking at my back, I guess, then I hear her walking down the hall. I feel like such a hypocrite. People are being so nice to me, and in my heart

I know I'm as bad as the guy everybody hates. The guy who's in jail. The guy who doesn't deserve to live.

I put on clean jeans and a fresh T-shirt. I've never been fat, but I'm really skinny now. And weak. Before the accident I'd get surges of energy, like I could leap tall buildings or some other kind of Superman crap. Now I barely have the energy to put one foot in front of the other, even though the doctor says I'm physically able to do anything I want but run track.

Between my mom and my grandma they've practically pushed me out the door to go to the Sandoval's house tonight. I don't want to go, but I don't have the energy to fight it, either. When I walk in and get a whiff of beans cooking in the big pot on the stove, it's as if nothing has happened. Mrs. Sandoval turns from the sink where she's cutting up tomatoes, wipes her hands on her apron and gives me a long, tight hug.

"We miss you," she says, looking at me in a questioning way. "Go look at Gabriel's cards," she says, leading me to the living room and pointing to a display of cards on the mantel, like a Christmas display, except these are all in light pastel colors, not the bright colors of Christmas. She scoops them up and hands them to me, then pulls me down next to her on the couch.

"Read them to me," she says, sitting back and closing her eyes.

The cards say things like, "Our prayers are with you in your time of loss," and "Deepest Sympathy," and there are lots of Bible verse cards.

"It helps to know so many people loved Gabriel. They did, didn't they?"

"Everybody liked Gabe," I say, remembering the time Gabe and I were hit up by some guys from Eighth Street—gang bangers. They'd asked us where we were from and Gabe made some smart remark that I thought would get us killed. But they laughed, shook hands around, and Gabe and I went on our way.

Mrs. Sandoval sighs. "Every day I go to early mass. I pray for him. I know his soul is already with God, but I pray for him anyway. It helps me keep him close."

When I ask about Gabe's grandparents, his mom tells me they've gone home to Mexico for a visit.

"It's been hard for them, too," she says.

Hector comes in from the garage, wiping his greasy hands on a rag. He starts to sit down next to his mom but she puts both hands on his butt and gives him a shove. "Not until you clean up," she says. They laugh and he goes into the bathroom to shower.

Monique yells from the kitchen, "Papá's home." Mrs. Sandoval goes to the door to greet her husband. Gabe used to say his family was the poorer Mexican equivalent to the Cosbys.

I'm beginning to relax, but when I sit down at the table with the family I'm faced with what's missing. I want to run away.

Hector starts talking about how the guy who hit us is due to be sentenced in a few days. "I hope they throw away the key," he says. "I'm gonna go down there and sit in on that session. When I see him in the courtroom I'm going to remind him that he murdered my brother."

Mr. Sandoval looks at him, sadly. "Spreading misery won't bring Gabriel back," he says.

"No. But I want justice!" Hector says.

"No, you want vengeance," his father says. "It's not the same."

"Shhh," Mrs. Sandoval says. "Dinner is a happy time."

Everyone is quiet for a while, then Mr. Sandoval turns to me and asks, "Are you getting your strength back, Paul?"

"Yeah, I guess."

"You look a lot better than the last time I saw you, except you're nothing but skin and bones. You need more beans," he says, heaping another big spoonful onto my plate.

"My grandma keeps trying to feed me menúdo," I say, wrinkling my nose. I don't tell them what I do with the menúdo, though.

"Ai, M'ijo, la abuela knows what's good for you!" Mrs. Sandoval says.

Monique keeps watching me at dinner, and I remember what Gabe said about her being in love with me. I don't think she is anymore, though. How could she be? Not that I want her to be.

"Remember Mrs. Walker?" she asks Hector.

"How could I forget. I had to take freshman English twice because of her."

She does an imitation of Mrs. Walker, standing at the board, tight lipped, pigeon toed, demonstrating comma usage. That makes us all laugh. I can see she thinks it's a big deal that I'm laughing. Come to think of it, it is.

It's strange. Gabe was the one to clown around whenever there was any tension at dinner. Now Monique is being the clown, filling a small corner of the big empty space at this table.

After dinner Mrs. Sandoval asks me to come with her into Gabe's room.

"I sit in here sometimes," she says. "I feel him here, do you?"

I don't know what to say. How am I supposed to feel someone's presence when they're already dead? It's not like I believe in ghosts or anything.

"Ai, M'ijo, I pray for *you* every morning, too. I see some of the life has gone from you. I know your body was hurt very bad, but I pray for your heart."

"I hurt all over," I tell her. "I don't know what hurts the most."

I look around at Gabe's room, pretty much the way it was the last time I saw it, minus dirty clothes strewn all over. There's a prom picture of him and Angie on his dresser, and posters of practically every Salsa group that's ever made a record tacked all over the walls. There's even a poster on the ceiling. His track medals are stuck into a cork board, and there's a picture from the school newspaper showing me crossing the line in a state competition. His walkman is on the bed, like he's just tossed it there. I reach for it, to see what tape is in it, check out what the last song was that he ever heard, but then I pull away, preferring not to know.

"It is true what I told you in the hospital," his mother says.

"What?"

"He didn't die for nothing. Someone who didn't have long to

live now has a strong, healthy heart. Someone else now has healthy lungs. And a liver. The only thing Javier and I asked was that the liver not go to someone who'd ruined their own with alcohol—knowing what we knew about the driver who ran into you boys."

Man, I feel like such a fake, sitting here listening to all this, the part I had in Gabe's death sitting heavy inside me.

"We gave everything that could be used, except his eyes," Mrs. Sandoval says. "From the time he was a baby, I felt I could see into his soul through his deep, brown eyes. And the sparkle—always that made me smile, even when he was up to something he shouldn't have been. I was afraid that if we gave his eyes, I would be looking for that soul, that sparkle, in every stranger on the street. So his eyes are buried with him. Were we selfish?"

I can't answer. My chest is so filled with sorrow it feels as if it will burst. My eyes ache from holding back tears.

Mrs. Sandoval's cheeks are wet, but she laughs anyway. "Even his Achilles tendons are now a part of someone else. Can you imagine? Probably whoever got them is surprised to find themselves sprinting all over the place."

"I hope they're not on some eighty-year-old lady," I say, seeing some humor in the situation.

"I don't think they both went to the same person," she says.

"That's even worse," I say. "One leg is sprinting and the other is dragging along."

"Going in circles," she says.

We both laugh until we're gasping. Mrs. Sandoval lets one, covers her face in embarrassment, and we laugh even harder. Monique pokes her head into the room.

"What's so funny?" she says, with a half smile.

"You had to be there," I tell her.

I'm only on a home teaching plan for four weeks when the doctor releases me to return to regular classes. No P.E. yet, but everything else the same as before. I'm not supposed to be sitting around so much, but it's all I really feel like doing.

When Mom stops in front of the school on my first day back she asks, "Are you okay?"

"I guess."

"I'm sorry you're having such a hard time, Honey . . . I'm just so glad you're alive, but I know it's going to take some time for things to get back to normal."

"Normal?" I say.

"Paul, I'm sorry. Nothing I say to you seems to come out right anymore. I miss Gabe, too. Everybody does. But somehow life goes on."

God, I hate when people say that, like that's supposed to make everything all right.

It's weird, really weird, to be back at Hamilton High. First period, Algebra II, I'm lost. I try to concentrate, but it's like Mr. Horton is saying blah, blah, blah. Nothing makes sense. After class, Eric and I walk out together.

"When're you coming back to track?" he asks.

"I don't know. It's like a big effort to *walk*, much less run."

"Man, we suck right now without you and Gabe—maybe you could at least start practicing the baton pass with Tyler."

"Is he still fumbling?" I ask.

"I think he rubs grease on his fingers before every meet," Eric laughs. "I've been practicing with him, but not enough, I guess."

Eric walks on to his second period class and I go to my locker to get the notebook and texts which have been sitting there untouched for over a month. I stand in front of it, drawing a blank on my combination number. I try about ten times to open it, but I can't do it. I bang my hand hard against the locker. It doesn't help.

Down the hall I hear someone yell, "Oh, shit!" and it is Gabriel's voice. Crash! Metal crumples metal. Glass shatters. My heart pounds wildly with the spin and roll of the car. My face, hands, armpits drip sweat as I feel the emptiness in the seat beside me. I rest my head against the metal of my locker, waiting for the sirens, the lights, the pounding, spinning, sweating to stop. I am breathing hard and fast, like at the end of a race. I force myself to take regular, slow breaths, to come away from the accident, back to the present.

I walk to class, passing friends who call out to me. I nod my head, mutter hi, hurry on. In English, Mrs. Rosenbloom welcomes me back without complaining that I have no notebook or textbook. Before this all happened she would have given me a really hard time about coming to class unprepared. I've always liked this class, but now it's more blah, blah, blah. Desiree passes me a note asking me to meet her at her car at lunchtime. Yes, I nod. She smiles. Mrs. Rosenbloom sees but doesn't say anything. Talk about special treatment. That's weird, too.

Back out in the hall, I hear it again, "Oh, shit!" and the pictures roll to the accompaniment of my pounding heart, dripping sweat, dry mouth. I never realized how many times that phrase gets shouted in the halls of Hamilton High. It's practically as common as "How's it going?" Over and over again, "Oh, shit!" Over and over again—replay.

I put my trembling hands deep into my pockets and walk past my third period class and through the gate. The narc doesn't even bother to ask where I'm going. I walk through the back parking lot and out onto the sidewalk. It is two miles to my house— nothing to get tired over, but by the time I get home my legs are shaky and I'm winded. I go inside, thankful to find an empty house. I ease down across the bed, waiting for the numbing fog. I am still there when my mom gets home from work in the evening.

"How was it?" she says, sitting in the chair beside my desk.

"I didn't stay. I can't think right, Mom."

She moves over to where I'm stretched out, face down, across my bed. She sits beside me and starts rubbing my back like she used to do when I was a kid.

"You've got to keep trying, Paulie. Remember, Dr. Baines told you it would be hard to concentrate for a while, but it's important to keep working at it."

My grandma comes in, carrying a package of freshly made,

still warm tortillas.

"I stopped at Pedro's on my way home," she says. "Smell."

She unwraps the package and puts it down by my face. I turn over, suddenly realizing how long it's been since I've eaten. I take a tortilla from the package, roll it and start eating. My mom and grandma each take one, too, both smiling now. I follow them to the kitchen and open a soda while my grandma starts cooking chicken and my mom makes a salad.

After dinner I ask to borrow my mom's car. She looks at me, puzzled, but hands me the keys. "Don't be late," she says, then adds in a whisper, "Be careful."

I've not driven since that night, and my hands are damp against the steering wheel of my mom's Nissan. I back out of the driveway and go out of my way to avoid the corner of Fourth and Sycamore. It takes about twenty minutes to get to the cemetery. Everything is locked up, but the low fence is easy to climb. I remember where Gabe's aunt is buried because I came with the family a few times when they brought flowers. Gabe's grave is right next to hers, and the seam between the newly rolled-on grass and the stuff that's been there for a long time is still obvious. "Gabriel Miguel Sandoval" is chiseled into a white marble headstone and underneath that the dates of his birth and death, and then it says "Beloved son, brother, grandson, friend." Then there is a torch, like in the Olympics, and under that it says, "His flame lives on." What does that mean, anyway?

I sit on the damp grass, next to the headstone, thinking. Maybe it means that parts of him, his heart and liver and all that stuff, are still alive in whoever got them. Well, I'm glad that makes his mom and dad feel better, and I guess it's nice for the people who needed parts, but it doesn't do much for me. I'm not catching his flame.

Right under me, six feet they say, all locked up in a casket, is my best friend. And hc's there because of me. That's the truth. I can't run from it, the fog isn't thick enough to block it out. He's down there missing all of the things that made him work—his heart isn't even in there. His eyes are down there, but they probably don't look so good anymore. God. I wonder what his emptied-out body looks like.

"I'm sorry, Gabe. I didn't mean to let you ride with me without your seat-belt. I didn't mean for you to die," I say. And then all the sorrow that's been locked up inside me comes loose. Tears run down my cheeks and my nose is running all over the place, but I don't care. "I miss you, Gabe. Sometimes it seems like I should be dead, too, but then I see my mom and grandma, and your mom, too, and I know they've been hurt bad enough as it is . . . I'm all confused and bottled up and there's no one to talk to about it because you're the only one I ever really talked to . . ." I'm sitting there with my head resting in my hands, tears pouring down my cheeks, picturing Gabe below ground, when a noise behind me makes me jump. It's Hector. I wipe my eyes, embarrassed, but I see that his cheeks are wet with tears, too.

"What're you doing here?" he asks.

"I just wanted to come here," I say. "I can't explain it."

"Yeah," he sighs. "I come here every night."

"Do you think Gabe knows we're here—like maybe he's watching from heaven?"

"Hey, I don't know. That's my mom's department. I guess he could be, but I'd rather see him here with us right now."

We stand in silence for a few minutes, then I say goodbye to Hector. I walk back to the fence, climb over it, and reach into my pocket for the car keys. Not there. Now what? I look all around by the fence. It's not very well lit, but there's enough moonlight that I'd see the keys if they were there. They probably fell out of my pocket when I was sitting on the grass. I climb back over the fence and walk back to where Gabe is buried. I walk quietly, not wanting to disturb Hector. When I get close, I hear that he is talking to Gabe and crying. I stop, not knowing what to do. Maybe I should just wait until he's finished?

"God, Gabe. It's bad enough that you're gone, but that it's my fault? I'm not sure I can stand it."

His fault? I stand there, barely breathing.

"If I'd just gone to get the ice cream, like mom asked, none of this would have happened. But I was lazy, like dad accuses me of being, and I didn't want to be bothered."

He is crying like a little kid now, making those choking sounds.

"Mom told Dad it was her fault—if she had bought enough ice cream in the first place, you'd still be here. But I'm the one who sent you on an errand I was supposed to do myself," Hector says, and the sobbing starts again.

I walk over slowly to where he's sitting. "I'm sorry. I think I lost the car keys around here," I say.

He looks up, wiping his face. I sit down next to him.

"Listen, Hector, I couldn't help hearing some of what you were saying. It's not your fault."

"No! Everybody tells me that, but you can't deny it. If I'd gone for ice cream myself, Gabe wouldn't be dead and you wouldn't be walking around half-dead!"

"Maybe," I say. "But there's more to it than that." I tell him the whole story about that night—the story I keep trying not to think about.

"Two beers, even three over the whole afternoon and night—I don't think you can call that drunk."

"But don't you see? If I hadn't had those beers, I would have noticed that Gabe wasn't wearing his seat-belt. I'm sure of it. I'd never taken anyone anywhere in my car unless they were buckled up. Never before that night."

"He probably would have been killed, anyway," Hector says. "I saw your car before they junked it. The whole right side was jammed flat against the steering wheel. Really, it's amazing you're alive. But see, your car wouldn't even have been there when that guy went zooming through the red light if I'd gone to get the ice cream."

"Does your mom really think it's her fault?"

"I don't know. I just heard them talking. My dad says life is full of what ifs and they get in the way of living—we just have to go on."

I start searching around on the grass, near where I was sitting before.

"You're not going to find those keys tonight," Hector says. "C'mon, I'll take you home and you can get the other set."

Just as he says that, my hand touches cold metal and my simplest problem is solved. We go back to the fence together, climb over, get in our cars and drive home. I follow him all the way, glancing now and then at the back of his head, thinking about how he used to bully us when we were little, and how defenseless he seems now.

Mom is waiting by the window, watching for me, as I turn into our driveway. By the time I walk through the front door, she is on the couch, pretending to be involved in a TV program.

"Goodnight, Mom," I say, walking back to my room.

"I'll take you to school in the morning, on my way to work," she calls after me.

I don't think I'm going to school in the morning. I don't think I can hack it. But I'll wait and tell her that tomorrow, when she's in a hurry and won't have time to argue about it.

I pick up the practice baton from my dresser and hold it tight, thinking of the thousands of times Gabe and I passed it back and forth, trying to feel his presence in it, like his mom says she feels in his room. All I feel is the familiar weight and texture in the palm of my hand.

In my dream Gabe keeps passing the baton to me and I keep dropping it. I'm surprised, because usually it's the other way around. "Hang on!" he keeps yelling. I yell back, "Buckle! Buckle!" but he laughs and hands the baton off to me again. It slips away. Then suddenly I'm in a distance race. My feet are like lead. I'm moving as fast as I can, but the finish line keeps getting farther and farther away. Gabe is at the other end, laughing, urging me on, but he keeps getting farther and farther away, too, until he is only a dot on the horizon. I fall face down on the track, heavy, unable to move.

"Get up!" a voice urges in my ear. It is Gabe's voice. "Run," he says. "You're the endurance guy, remember? I'm just the sprinter. My race was exciting, fast, but it's over. You've barely started yours." He laughs again.

A lightness returns. I get to my hands and knees.

"Get up, Paul," he says, "get up," over and over, until his voice fades and my mother's voice picks up the rhythm, "Get up, Paul. Get up," she says, shaking me gently.

I roll over on my back and take a deep breath. Mom opens the blinds. "It's a nice, sunny day," she says. "I'm going to jump in the shower now. Get yourself a bite to eat and we'll leave in about thirty minutes."

Maybe I should go to school today after all. I rummage around in my top dresser drawer. Like with the keys last night, I'm in luck this morning. I find my wallet, and the torn slip of paper that has my locker combination on it. I take a quick shower and start getting dressed.

When I pull my pants on, though, something feels heavy, out of balance. I reach into my right pocket and pull out the baton I'd held in my hand last night. But I put it back on the dresser! I know I did. How did it get in my pocket? Did I sleepwalk? I've never done that before. I sit down on my bed, holding the baton, remembering my dream.

"Ready?" Mom asks, standing in the doorway.

"Did you hear anything last night after I went to bed?" I ask.

"No, like what?"

"Well, like maybe I was sleepwalking or something?"

"No," she says, shaking her head, looking puzzled. "Why?"

"Oh, nothing. I was just wondering."

I put the baton back in my pocket, walk past her to the kitchen and grab a couple of breakfast bars. "Let's go," I say.

Today, when I hear "Oh, shit!" in the halls, I immediately change the word "shit" to "shinola" in my head. That sounds really weird, I know, but in Peer Counseling, when we were trying to clean up our language, Woodsy suggested we say "fudge" instead of the usual "f" word, and "shinola" instead of "shit."

It helps a little. One time "Oh, shit" brings the replay of the accident in all its intensity, but the rest of the time "shinola" works.

Algebra II still doesn't make much sense to me this morning, but it's maybe a little better than yesterday. *I'm* a little better than yesterday.

I catch up with Desiree before English. "Sorry about yesterday," I say.

"I waited for you for twenty minutes," she says, her eyes flashing anger.

"Want to try again today?" I ask.

"No way," she says.

I shrug. She doesn't seem very important to me anymore.

I reach into my pocket and touch the baton, wondering how it got there this morning. All day I feel the weight of it in my pocket. Sixth period I go out to the track.

"Hey, Valdez," Coach Sawyer says, walking over to me and shaking my hand. "We need you. Are you getting back in shape? How're you doing?"

"Okay, I guess."

"Ready to run?"

"The doctor hasn't released me for that yet, but I thought maybe I could help coach exchanges between Tyler and one of the other guys."

"Great. Tyler needs all the coaching he can get," Coach laughs, then he gets serious. "That was a rotten break for you guys," he says. "What a waste."

"Yeah," I say.

"I heard someone got Gabe's Achilles tendons," Coach says.

"Yeah," I smile. I tell him about the conversation I had with Gabe's mom about someone running in circles because one side would be so fast. We laugh. Coach calls Tyler and we start practicing. It feels good to be outside, doing something. I run just enough to be moving when Tyler reaches for the baton, but that's enough to wind me.

After school I go to In-N-Out Burger with Eric and Tyler and Manuel. We sit in Eric's car for a long time, eating and talking. When I get home I'm so tired I stretch out on the couch and fall asleep. But it's a good sleep, not a wishing-for-fog sleep.

After Mom gets home I borrow the car again and go to the cemetery. Hector is already there. I tell him about my weird dream, and the really weird thing with the baton in my pocket.

"You probably put it there and forgot," he says, but I know better.

"I dream about Gabe sometimes, too. He's always laughing in my dreams. I think that's a good sign, don't you? Like he doesn't hold anything against me?"

"Gabe never held anything against anyone," I say. "He'd always say how everyone makes mistakes so why be all uptight about anything so natural as some stupid mistake?"

Hector and I are quiet for a while, thinking our own thoughts.

"I guess we don't have to hold anything against us either," he says. "Like I don't need to feel guilty about the ice cream, and you don't need to feel guilty about the beer."

"I'll always feel guilty about the beer," I say. "I'll always wonder 'what if?' But I think he was right, in my dream. He sprinted through life and finished early, and I've got to work on endurance. I can't help thinking 'what if?' but I can't give up before I'm even halfway into the race, either."

We talk a while longer, then walk back across the cemetery to our cars. I drive to the corner of Fourth and Sycamore and pull over to the curb. I sit there until my breathing slows. I can't be running away from things, avoiding things.

So now I can drive past this corner. I can hear "Oh, shit," without freaking out. I can be doing something useful in track. It doesn't bring my friend back and it doesn't take away the what ifs, but it's helping to ease me back into the race. Gabe would want it. I want it.

For Ethan and Me

*"I can't have another baby.
I can barely take care of Ethan."*

CHAPTER

1

I can't believe this! I look at the pink form, as if looking at it again will change the words. There it is, my name, Christina Calderon, and a check in the box that says *PREGNANCY POSITIVE.* I sit on the bench outside the Family Planning Clinic, waiting for the 4:30 bus, crying. God! How could I have let this happen? Since I had my baby, Ethan, almost two years ago, I've been practically living the life of a nun. Then I let myself get carried away. Once! Just one time! And I'm pregnant. What an idiot.

I feel sick, not only from being pregnant, but from being stupid. I hope I don't throw up. I keep having to swallow, and I'm all sweaty. By the time I get off the bus and walk two blocks to my job at The Gap, the wave of nausea has passed. Usually I only throw up in the mornings, unless I catch a whiff of cigarette smoke or the smell of greasy food, then watch out. It's a good thing I don't work at Burger King.

"Hey, you green-eyed Latin beauty," Alex says as I shove my bookbag under the counter. "Let's grab some bills from the cash drawer, hop a plane to Jamaica, and live the rest of our lives on love."

"I'm not in a joking mood, Alex," I say.

"Who's joking?"

I shine him on. He's cute, I guess, if you like the surfer look—blond hair, blue eyes, kind of an athletic build. I think he's about nineteen. There's always some girl hanging around, pretending to be looking at clothes but really trying to get Alex to notice her, which is usually not too difficult. He's always flirting with me. But he's not my type. Besides, men—they mean trouble to me.

Tiffany, who is a friend of mine from school and also is the assistant manager, comes over to talk to us. She's kind of chubby, in a cute sort of way. She's got short black hair and big dark eyes. She and I are in Peer Counseling together. That's my favorite class because it deals with real life. My other favorite school thing is being a teacher's aide in the hearing-impaired classes. I want to work with deaf kids when I finish college.

"So far, things have been slow this afternoon," Tiffany says. "Justin will be back in the stockroom unless things get busy later. Christy, you stay at the cash register and Alex, would you straighten out the sale tables and check to be sure the jeans and T-shirts are in order on the shelves?"

"No problem," Alex says.

I wish it would get so busy I wouldn't have time to think, but hardly anyone's in the store tonight. Time drags. I reach deep into my pocket and feel the pregnancy form. I want to take it out and look at it again, but that's dumb. I know what it says.

Suddenly I jump about two feet. "Don't do that!" I scream at Alex. He's got this habit of sneaking up behind people and poking them in the ribs. I hate it.

"Gotcha," he laughs.

"Grow up," I say.

"What's eating you?" he says. "You're a bigger grouch than usual tonight."

I feel tears filling my eyes and I look away. I hate being called a grouch. Some of my so-called friends at school started calling me that last year, because I never went out with them anymore. I tried to explain that it's not that I'm a grouch, it's just that I've got a lot, I mean *a lot*, of responsibility with my baby. Some people don't understand that, though. I know I didn't, until after Ethan was born.

When Alex takes his break, Tiffany comes over to where I'm straightening a rack of shirts.

"Are you okay?" she asks.

"Fine," I say, looking away.

"You looked like you were ready to cry when Alex was teasing you. He doesn't mean anything by it, you know," she says.

"It's not just Alex," I say.

"But something's wrong," Tiffany says. "I'm your friend, remember?"

Sometimes I can't stand it when people are nice to me. I go along, keeping everything inside, cold and hard, and then somebody shows they care, and all my locked-up tears start pouring out. Right now, I can't help it. I start sobbing.

"Hey," Tiffany says, moving closer to me. "What is it?"

Then this dad and his sullen-looking son come to the counter to pay for some jeans. Tiffany rings them up while I walk over to a deserted part of the store. How embarrassing for a customer to see me crying!

When Tiffany finishes the sale, I hear her call to Alex and tell him to take over for a while. Then she comes over to where I'm standing, takes me by the arm, and walks with me back to the employees' lounge.

"It might help to talk, and you know I won't blab about whatever it is that's bothering you," she says, handing me a tissue.

I nod. I know from Peer Counseling she doesn't go around gossiping about people's problems—she respects confidentiality, like we're all supposed to, but not everyone does.

We sit at the big round table that's got doughnut crumbs and hardened refried beans on it because some people never clean up after themselves. I'm crying my guts out. I wish I could cry out the little seed that's started growing inside of me.

Tiffany sits with me, not saying anything. Finally, I take the pregnancy form from my pocket and slide it across the table to her. She reads it once, then again.

"You're pregnant?" she asks.

I nod.

"And you're not happy?"

"Do I seem happy to you?" I gasp out between sobs. Then, I don't know why, I guess I'm a psycho or something, but I start laughing. Tiffany looks at me kind of funny, for an instant, then she starts laughing, too. Pretty soon we're both laughing so hard we can hardly catch our breath. Then I get serious again.

"God, Tiff, I can't have another baby. I can barely take care of Ethan."

She slides the pregnancy positive paper back to me.

"What does your boyfriend say?" she asks.

"He's not even my boyfriend," I tell her.

She looks at me, wide-eyed, but says nothing.

"Do you think I'm a slut?" I whisper, afraid of her answer.

"No," she says.

"I've always thought that about girls who get pregnant from someone who's not even their boyfriend."

"Me, too," Tiffany says. "But I know you're a good person. I would never think you're a slut."

My tears start again. I can't control them.

"We can use some help out here!" Justin yells from the hallway.

"I'll go," Tiffany says, touching my shoulder as she walks past me.

I go into the restroom, splash cold water on my face, and try to look better. I take a bunch of deep breaths, then I go back out front. People are lined up at the cash register. For the next hour, until closing time, we are very busy and I don't have time to dwell on my problems.

After work, Tiffany and I sit on the bench in front of the store, waiting for our rides.

"So what happened?" she asks. "All that safe sex stuff . . ."

I know what she means. My senior project in Peer Counseling includes giving safe sex talks to ninth grade health classes. Tiffany is working on the same project. We go to classrooms with a big "Safer Sex" bag filled with condoms, foam, a diaphragm, a cervical cap, you name it. If it cuts the chances of pregnancy or AIDS, it's in our bag.

"You weren't raped, were you?" she asks in a whisper.

"No. It's my own fault. That's what's so stupid. The first time I got pregnant, I sort of let it happen. My boyfriend then, Jeff, didn't seem to love me the way he had in the beginning."

"He's the guy who was on the debate team when we were sophomores, right?"

"Right."

"I remember seeing him and that black guy, Dashan, at an assembly. I thought they were both so cool."

"Yeah. I thought so, too. I was really dependent on Jeff. I didn't get along with my dad, who's the bossy type, and I couldn't stand the way my mom let him push her around. My sister, Maria—you know Maria?"

"Hangs out with the Eighth Street Cholas?"

"Yeah, that's my sister all right. She's one of the biggest brats ever invented—so I didn't have what you'd call a satisfying, fun, family life. When Jeff and I got together he gave me a lot I really needed. He was fun, and loving, especially at first . . . Anyway, when he started seeming less interested in me I got really scared. I kept looking for signs that would reassure me that we'd always be together. I know it sounds totally bizarre, but if I put catsup on my french fries and then he put catsup on his french fries, that meant we would stay together. Sometimes, if he didn't put catsup on his fries, I would dump some on, like that would *make* us stay together. What it did was annoy him in the extreme."

Tiffany laughs.

"What can I say? I've already admitted how stupid I was. But talk about stupid! I started thinking that if I happened to get pregnant, that would really mean we'd always be together—a baby from both of us would be like a sign from God, or fate, or something. So I stopped taking the pill, and I didn't tell Jeff."

"You stopped taking the pill, and he thought you were still on it?" Tiffany says, looking at me like she can't believe what I'm saying. She and I sort of knew each other back then, but we didn't get to be real friends until I started working at The Gap.

"Here's what I thought in my dumb little fifteen-year-old brain," I tell her. "If I didn't get pregnant, then maybe it wasn't meant to be, but if I did, we would stay together, for certain. That's what I thought. I thought I'd get away from my bossy dad, and that Jeff and his mom would take care of me and the baby at their house. What a joke!"

"I have a friend from junior high school who got pregnant to get away from her house. It only made things worse," Tiffany says.

"Me, too. Jeff was so angry that I'd let myself get pregnant that any chance I had of keeping him was lost. Now I know you can't trick people into loving you, but back then I was lonely and desperate . . . But God, I can't believe I've let myself get pregnant now!"

"Maybe there's a mistake," Tiffany says.

I shake my head. "I know what it feels like to be pregnant, and I'm definitely pregnant."

Tiffany's mom pulls up in a bright red sports car, a Miata I think, and honks the horn.

"See you tomorrow," Tiffany says as she gets in the car and waves back to me.

After she's gone I feel lonely, and kind of embarrassed about telling her all that stuff.

CHAPTER

2

It's 9:30 by the time my dad comes to get me. He has Ethan in the car with him.

"Mommy! Mommy!" Ethan yells, leaning as far out of the car seat as he can, reaching his arms toward me.

"Hey, lover baby," I say, leaning in and nuzzling his soft, sweet-smelling neck. We both giggle, and for an instant I forget everything else. I slide into the back seat, beside him, so I can play with him on the way home.

"He wouldn't go to sleep," my dad announces in a tone that means it's my fault.

I ruffle Ethan's hair. He grabs my hand with his own dirty, sticky hand.

"Did he get a bath yet?" I ask.

"No. Your mother went to bed early. She was tired," Dad says, as if that's my fault, too.

I look at the back of his head, feeling anger well up, knowing it's best to keep my mouth shut. But couldn't he even give his own grandson a bath? He's probably been watching some mindless ball game all evening long, barely paying attention to Ethan. My mom says he gets tired easy because he's older, but she's always making excuses for him. I think his day's easier than mine.

This morning I was up at six—got ready for school, then got Ethan up and dressed, fed him breakfast, packed his Lion King bookbag, and caught the school van with him. I got him settled at the Infant Center, and then caught the van to Hamilton High. Besides my regular classes I had to do a Safer Sex presentation to a ninth grade health class, which was fine, but it took up my whole lunch period. Then I had to keep my appointment at the clinic, rush to work, and here I am now, with at least another hour of stuff with Ethan before I can get him settled down. It will be ten o'clock at the earliest before I can even start my homework. Then up at six tomorrow morning for more of the same.

As far as I can see, all my dad has to do is get dressed in the morning, go to work, come home and flop down in his chair, and start bossing people around and expecting to be waited on. But then I think about how Darlene's dad kicked her out of the house when she was pregnant, and how he won't even see her baby. I guess I shouldn't complain.

Sometimes I wonder if things will ever be any easier for me. Like, will I ever get out from under my parents and into a life of my own? Most of my friends are all excited about going away to college. My grades are good enough to get me into lots of different places, probably even with some financial help, but I can't figure out how to live in a dormitory with Ethan. And since Jeff and I have joint custody, I can't very well move away with Ethan.

Anyway, my life is a lot more complicated than Tiffany's, or Alex's, or anyone else I know who's my age, except for the other girls in the Teen Moms program. Some of them are a lot worse off than I am. At least I know what I want to do, like for a career, and even if Jeff and I aren't together anymore, we share responsibility for Ethan pretty well. Some of my friends who have babies don't get any help from anyone.

I walk in the door carrying Ethan and my bookbag, which weighs about a ton. Maria, who is fourteen years old, always seems mad at something. She's watching TV, and she doesn't even look up when I say hi to her. I walk straight past her, down the hall and into the bathroom where I start Ethan's bath. He loves it, and even after ten minutes of splashing and playing he still doesn't want to get out. Only when I drain the water out will he lift his arms to me and let me take him out of the tub. I wrap him in a towel and carry him into the bedroom that he and I share. I dry all of his cracks and crevices and rub baby powder on his sweet, brown body.

He's got Jeff's features—a thin nose, dimple in his chin, kind of a high forehead, but he's got my coloring—medium dark skin and dark hair. Except for the color of his eyes and his thin nose, he looks Mexican, like my family. But his last name is Browning. I hope he doesn't develop an identity crisis later on.

I read stories I hope will make him want to go to sleep, like *Good Night Moon,* and *Bedtime Bear*, and *Sleepytime Mouse.* Then he turns over on his side and sticks his thumb in his mouth. I rub his back for a while and then, finally, I hear the deeper breathing that lets me know he's asleep.

I take my books to the kitchen table and start on tomorrow's assignments. My mind wanders as I'm reading a short story for English—it's about some shoe salesman and right now I couldn't care less. What am I going to do? I keep thinking—thinking of all the responsibilities I have right now, thinking I can't do it. No way can I manage two babies. What am I going to do? God, I wish I could go back and erase that one senseless night with Benny.

I think about Karla, who has a boy a little older than Ethan and a baby about three months old. She's dropped out of school, she's always depressed, and she yells at her kids all the time. She wears the same clothes practically every day, and she already looks like she's about forty years old. I don't want that.

I can't have another baby! Not yet. There's only one thing to do—the thing I never thought I *would* do. But would it be murder? I was raised to believe it's murder to end a pregnancy. I mean, I *am* Catholic. Isn't that what I'm supposed to believe?

But now, when it's just a cluster of cells? Is *that* murder? If I don't have the baby, will I burn in hell? But if I do have another baby, my life will be totally messed up. Which means Ethan's life will be messed up, too.

My dad would go more nuts this time than he did the first time. He thinks I'm all pure again, living a life of celibacy. Which I was except for that one unchangeable night. And my mom—she's always dragging around as it is. As much as she loves Ethan, I know he wears her out. Another baby in this house? Forget it.

One thing for sure, Benny's never going to know he got me pregnant. Next year I'm going to Hamilton Heights City College, and then in two years I'll transfer to Cal State Northridge for a degree in Deaf Studies, just like I've planned all along. I'm not going to let this one mistake spoil everything.

On Wednesday morning Tiffany and I do a Safe Sex talk. I feel like such a hypocrite, standing up in front of a bunch of ninth graders and talking to them about the importance of using foam and condoms, just after I've thrown up in the bathroom because I'm pregnant, because I *didn't* use foam and a condom when I should have.

After the class is over Tiffany and I walk down to the gym together. At first we talk about work, and the end-of-the-year party in Peer Counseling. Then she asks about my problem.

"I can't have another baby. It would mess up too many lives, including mine."

"So are you having an abortion?"

I nod, struck silent by the word. I hadn't thought that word yet.

"You're sure?" she says.

"God, I've thought about it up and down and backwards and forwards. It's the only thing to do."

Tiffany gets this far-away look in her eyes.

"Do you think I'm awful?" I ask.

"No. I just think it's a hard decision. When will you do it?" she asks.

"I'm going to the clinic today to get an appointment."

"Well, let me know when you get scheduled. I'll take you. It's better not to have to ride a bus on that day," she says.

"Thanks," I sigh. "No one else knows I'm doing this, or even that I'm pregnant."

"Aren't you even telling your boyfriend though?"

"He's not really my boyfriend," I remind her. Then we go off in different directions to our separate classes. I walk along the hallway, thinking about the guy who is not my boyfriend, and who will never know he got me pregnant. I can still hardly believe that it happened. Here's the thing.

Benny and I have been good friends, only friends, for a long time. After Ethan was born, when I was intensely depressed, Benny would stop by every day with some silly joke or story— anything to make me laugh. I don't know how I would have managed to get through that time if Benny hadn't been there for me.

Anyway, about a month ago, or maybe more like six weeks, Benny was waiting on my front porch when I got home from work. He's been stationed in South Carolina, so I was definitely surprised to see him.

"Let's go for a ride," he said. "I have a lot I want to talk to you about."

I checked inside. Ethan was already asleep. I gave him a quick kiss on his baby cheek, grabbed a sweatshirt, told my parents where I was going, and went back outside where Benny was waiting, leaning against his car.

My friend Kim is always wanting me to set her up with Ben. She thinks he's Mr. Studly, with his army muscles and his regulation haircut. He *is* sort of handsome, in an army way. I asked him about Kim once, but he wasn't interested.

But back to the night I'm remembering, the night I wish had never happened. We drove about ten miles up toward Mt. Wilson, then parked in a wooded area near the edge of a cliff. We rolled down the windows so we could smell the pine trees, and sat looking at the lights—pointing out what we could identify, like the Arco Towers and the Bonaventure Hotel. Then Benny reached behind him and pulled a couple of wine coolers out of a styrofoam ice chest.

"Celebrate with me," he said, taking the cap off two bottles and handing one to me. He clicked bottles with me, then took a long swallow from his.

"Celebrate what?" I asked.

"I get an all-expense-paid trip to a Caribbean Island." He tipped his bottle back and took another gulp. "C'mon, drink up. We're celebrating," he said with a smile.

I didn't understand what Ben was talking about when he told me he was getting a trip to a Caribbean Island, until he used the words "shipping out." Then I got it.

"It's a mess down there," he said. "Someone's got to straighten things out, and I guess it's got to be Uncle Sam and the boys."

I laughed, like I always did when Ben was sounding like John Wayne, but he didn't laugh with me, he just clicked bottles with me again.

I don't much like wine coolers, or beer, or any of that stuff. To me it's like drinking cough syrup. I took a sip anyway, just because Benny wanted me to. Benny downed his drink in about three giant swallows.

"We may see combat," he said. He opened another bottle for each of us and smiled at me. "Catch up," he said.

I took another few swallows, and then it began to taste pretty good. We sat there like that, not saying much, gazing at the lights, drinking wine coolers, for a long time.

"Are you scared?" I asked.

"No, not scared. But it's really made me think about things."

Then, after another long silence, Benny took my face in his hands and turned it toward him, giving me a slow, gentle kiss. I was so shocked I didn't even do anything, like push him away, or draw back from him.

"I've wanted that so long," he said, looking at me with such warmth that I had to look away. "I tried to tell you last time I saw you. Remember that night we walked around the golf course?"

"I remember," I said.

"I wanted so much to kiss you, and to tell you how I felt. But I was afraid. And then, when I got back to the base I wrote you about eight letters, but I kept tearing them up because none of them sounded right. But now that I'm shipping out, I've got to tell you. I love you, Christy," he said in a whisper. "I've loved you for a long time."

I could hardly believe what I'd just heard. He pulled me toward him.

"Marry me before I leave. Will you?"

I was stunned by the question.

"Will you?" he repeated.

"Benny . . ."

"Don't say no yet," he said, pulling me close to him. "I've got it all figured out. We can get the blood tests tomorrow and get married on Monday. You can finish up at Hamilton High. By that time I should be back from the little island skirmish and we can get housing on the base. Say yes," he pleaded. "There's a great little playground in the married compound. There would be lots of kids for Ethan to play with."

I pulled away from him and sat back in my seat, looking at the downtown lights, trying to figure out what to say. Finally I told him I wasn't ready to get married—that my plans for my life didn't include marriage for a long time.

"Not ready to get married to anyone, or just to me?" he asked.

"Not to anyone."

Benny reached for the wine coolers and opened two more.

I sipped at my drink, to keep my hands busy, to keep something in front of me so Ben wouldn't pull me close to him again. I was trying hard to decide what to say, but I was having trouble thinking. My head was spinning.

"You're my best friend, Benny. I love you like a brother," I finally told him.

"I don't want you to love me like a brother," he said, so loud it scared me. "I want you to love me like a man. I need to know I can come home to you. If I end up dying under some coconut tree, I want my last thought to be that you love me. I mean *really* love me," he said. Then he covered his face with his hands and began to cry in a sad, soft way.

Benny's definitely not the crying type. I didn't know what to do. I thought how he would soon be risking his life, and that he needed me, and how he'd been there for me when I needed him. My heart melted.

"Ben," I said, putting my arms around him. "It will be all right. Everything's going to be all right."

He clung to me, his head against my shoulder. I patted and rubbed his back, comforting him in the same way I comfort Ethan when he's hurt. I kissed the top of his head and wiped the tears from his face. It seemed natural, sisterly. Then, maybe it was the wine, or the stars, I don't know what. But something changed in me and Ben must have felt it. He kissed me lightly on the neck. I turned toward him and he kissed my mouth, gently at first and then with more force. I felt his tongue pushing at my lips, and I parted them for him.

Suddenly I couldn't get enough of Ben. I wanted him to kiss me harder, hold me tighter, get closer, closer. My fuzzy head was telling me to slow down, but my body wasn't listening. Somehow we were in the back seat, grappling with each other's clothes, frantic with desire. The moment Ben came inside me I sobered, but it was too late then. He held me for a long time while I cried without words.

"I'll be all right. Don't worry," he said. How could I tell him I was crying for me, not for him?

"Will you marry me, now?" he asked, as if having sex changed everything.

"No," I said.

"But at least I know now you love me."

I didn't contradict him. I let him think that, knowing he would be leaving in days and that it would be a long time before I saw him again. But I felt awful—dishonest. I'm pretty sure it wouldn't have happened if I hadn't been drinking those wine coolers. But that's no excuse. In a way it just makes things worse. Like I was *doubly* stupid instead of just stupid in *one* way.

So now I'm throwing up every morning, and getting ready to make arrangements for an abortion. And in spite of what Tiffany said, I'm still wondering if this makes me a slut.

After school, at the clinic, I go in for a consultation, fill out all the necessary forms, and get an appointment for the following Saturday.

3

Tiffany picks me up at eight on the appointed day. I've told my mom I have to be at school for special college entrance tests, which in reality I took months ago. I hate lies, but what can I do? Right now my whole life feels like a lie anyway because Benny still thinks maybe I love him. I can't bring myself to write him when he's in danger and add heartbreak to his problems, can I?

On the way to the clinic I start talking non-stop, I guess because I'm nervous.

"I'm only about five weeks pregnant," I tell Tiffany. "It's just a little blob of cells right now, not really a baby."

"It's good to do it now," Tiffany assures me.

"It's not even two inches long yet, no arms or legs—just a blob," I say.

Tiffany nods, her eyes on the road ahead.

"When I went in for my consultation, and to get my appointment, the nurse said that the vacuum things . . ."

"Aspiration." Tiffany supplies the word for me.

"Yeah. The vacuum aspiration abortions they do in the first trimester are safer than tonsillectomies or circumcisions . . . I haven't felt it move yet. I don't want to feel it move," I say. "The nurse told me it wouldn't be too painful. I wonder exactly how painful it will be."

"Do you want to change your mind?" Tiffany asks.

"Oh, no. I've been thinking about this all the time since I knew I was pregnant. No matter how many times I go over it in my head, this is the answer I come up with."

"It probably won't be too painful," she says. "Mine wasn't."

I'm totally surprised. I mean, Tiffany and I have been school and work friends for a while, but not the kind of friends that hang out together all the time and tell each other *everything*. It's just since that night at work when I told her I was pregnant that we've started talking about personal stuff. And now that I think of it, I've done most of the talking. I guess I've been so caught up in my own problem I've not been thinking about anyone else.

"You're surprised," she says.

"Yeah. I thought . . . I mean, it seems like maybe you would be one of those saving-herself-for-marriage kinds. Not a prude or anything, but just maybe not into sex."

She laughs.

I think about how I wasn't into sex except for that one wine cooler night. I wonder if that's what happened with Tiffany. "You'd be amazed to hear some of the other girls from Hamilton who've had abortions. It's like the deep dark secret that no one can talk about."

"It's embarrassing," I say.

"And maybe shameful?" she says.

"Maybe. I don't think so, but I guess a lot of other people do."

"Look," she says, as we turn the corner near the clinic.

There is a crowd and two police cars. A man, older than my father, is carrying a big, hand-lettered sign that says "Legalized murder done here." Police are keeping people clear of the walk up to the clinic door. As we get closer I hear some of the crowd chanting, "Abortion is murder. Abortion is murder."

Why can't these people mind their own business?

Tiffany pulls close to the curb and lets me out. "I'll come back and get you when you're finished—I'll get here about eleven.

You can call my beeper if you need me sooner."

"Thanks," I say. Then I put my head down and run past the jeering crowd to the doorway and into the waiting room. I sign in, then sit down and open the book I've brought to read. I can't concentrate.

"Don't you hate those bastards?" a woman next to me says, jerking her head in the direction of the protesters.

"I don't even know who they are," I say.

"I hate their guts. 'Specially the men who don't know shit about having babies." Her eyes flash anger. She is probably forty, real skinny, and her hair is bleached white.

"I know their type, too," she tells me. "They'll go home and get drunk and beat up on their wives, maybe their kids, too. Bastards!"

Then her whole attitude changes. "What's your name, Honey?" she asks me in a kindly manner.

"Christy," I say.

"I'm Yvonne," she says. "Nice to meet you." She extends her hand to me and we shake hands.

"How old are you?"

"Seventeen," I tell her.

"Ain't life a bitch?" she says.

The chanting is louder now. "Abortion is murder. Abortion is murder." Over and over again.

Yvonne walks over to the door, flings it open, and yells "Shut up, you dirty bastards!"

A policewoman lunges at her and pushes her back inside. The receptionist and someone else, a nurse or counselor or someone, hurry over.

"This doesn't help," the policewoman says, still gripping Yvonne by the arm.

"I know," the receptionist says. "It won't happen again."

Now Yvonne is chanting, "Dirty bastards, dirty bastards, dirty bastards" the way some people chant Hail Marys.

"Come back here and sit with me," the other clinic worker says, taking Yvonne by the arm and leading her down the hall.

"Bring Christy, too," she says. "She's my new little friend—seventeen."

"Okay, come on, Christy, if you want," the woman says, and I follow them down the hall, not wanting to hurt the skinny lady's feelings. While we're waiting for the doctor, Yvonne tells me she's HIV positive. "You know what the chances are of my baby eventually ending up with AIDS?" she asks.

"No," I say.

"Plenty," she says. "I wouldn't put no innocent kid through that. Those bastards out there, they wouldn't care. They wouldn't be around to help, you can bet your life on that! . . . So what's your story?" she asks.

"Well . . ." Just then Yvonne's number is called and she goes back to the examination room. I'm glad I don't have to tell her my story. Instead I remind myself of all the hurt and difficulty that would result from me having another baby. I remind myself that I'm doing this not just for me, but also for Ethan and my mom and dad. Even, in a way, for Benny. He deserves more love than I could offer him. When he gets a baby, it should be with someone who loves him a lot. Most of all though, I'm doing it for Ethan, so I can be a good mother to him, and make a life for us both.

About twenty minutes later my number is called. I feel all shaky inside as I follow a nurse into another room. She tells me to use the bathroom, then come back, which I do. I put on one of those hospital gown things and lie on my back on the examining table with my feet in the stirrups. I hate this! My palms are all sweaty and I feel like I can hardly catch a breath.

"Relax," the nurse says. Easy for her to say, but I take a deep breath and exhale slowly, trying not to be so tense.

The doctor comes into the room, introduces himself, checks my chart, washes his hands, puts on sterile gloves and examines me.

"You may feel a little cramping, Christy," he says. "It won't last long. Try not to tighten up."

I close my eyes and think of Ethan at home with my mom,

probably eating a peanut butter and jelly sandwich and drinking apple juice while she works in the kitchen. Or maybe she's helping him find sow bugs outside. He loves to do that. I love him so much. I want so much for him to have a good life.

I know what is happening. I read the pamphlet the nurse gave me before, and I looked at the pictures. The doctor is putting a tube up into my uterus. The tube is connected to this aspirator thing which is going to suck stuff out. Yuck.

Just as I'm picturing Ethan searching under the hibiscus bush for bugs, I feel a sharp cramp, more like a labor contraction. I gasp with pain.

"Relax, relax." The nurse takes my hand and holds it gently but firmly. "Breathe deeply, slowly," she says.

Another cramp, this one longer. I catch my breath. Bright colors, the color of pain, dance before my eyes.

"It's almost over," the doctor assures me.

I'm crying. I don't want to, but I can't help it. I feel the speculum eased out of me. They do something, clean me up I guess. I can't see and I don't ask.

"You did fine," the doctor says. "Stay here and rest for a few minutes. Just relax."

I'm so relieved, I cry even harder. The doctor leaves and the nurse hands me a tissue.

"Okay?" she asks.

I nod.

"I'll be back and check on you soon."

I feel crampy and nauseous. The nurse comes back and wipes my face with a cool cloth, then leaves again. After a while she returns, takes my blood pressure, listens to my heart, and checks for bleeding.

"Any more cramping?" she asks.

"No. I think it's stopped."

"Rest here for another twenty minutes or so, and then you can get dressed and be on your way. Take it easy this weekend, and avoid intercourse for at least three weeks."

"Years," I say.

She smiles. "I've heard that before," she says.

Tiffany is waiting for me. We walk out the back way, avoiding the demonstrators, then drive to Burger King and order burgers and fries at the drive-through window.

"You're white as a Barbie doll," Tiffany says, causing us to get a long-lasting case of the giggles.

We drive down a side street and park in the shade under a huge pepper tree. I pick at my burger, but I'm not really hungry.

Tiffany tells me about her abortion, two years ago. It was her older *cousin* who got her pregnant. Unbelievable! Well, I believe Tiffany. I just mean it's unbelievable what some people will do.

"I was on my way to being really messed up over that," she says. "But Peer Counseling has helped me a lot. Ms. Woods noticed I was having a hard time, and she got me started with this group of girls that share their problems. Maybe she guessed I'd had an abortion, I'm not sure. Anyway, knowing I wasn't alone helped a lot."

"Did you ever think you should have the baby instead of getting an abortion?" I asked.

"Yeah, I did. But my mom said it would be awful for the family. And now, I don't think I could handle a baby anyway. I don't see how you do it, and keep up with everything else."

"It's hard. Sometimes I get discouraged, like maybe I ought to forget about school and work and just get on welfare. But that's not really what I want."

We talk for a while longer, then Tiffany takes me home.

"Thank you," I say.

"I'm glad I could talk with you about my abortion, too," she says. "Hardly anyone knows except the girls in my group. Sometimes I feel phony, like everyone thinks I'm this virgin— like you did, and I'm not what I seem."

"That wasn't your fault at all," I remind her.

I see my mom standing at the window looking out.

"I've got to go," I say.

She smiles, and I think we'll be friends for a long time.

When I get into my house, Mom asks how the test went.

"It was okay," I say.

"Ay, Mija. You look so pale. I think you work too hard."

My poor mom. I've caused her a lot of worry and I hate that I lied to her about today— it would tear her apart if she knew I'd had an abortion. I can't do that to her. I put my arms around her.

"I love you, Mama," I say, just as Ethan comes running in from the other room, throwing his arms around my legs. I pick him up and walk out into the backyard with him. I'm so glad this is over. It's like I've been living in a fog since I first suspected I could be pregnant. Now I can pay attention to other things again. And I'll write to Benny tomorrow and tell him, in the best way I can possibly find, that we can only be friends. I can't stand that he thinks things are different between us than they really are.

"Bugs!" Ethan yells, having discovered a treasure. I go over and look at the tiny creatures with him. I kiss the back of his tender neck and feel tears gathering in my eyes. What a mix, of sorrow, shame, relief, mostly relief.

"Bear hug!" I say to Ethan.

"Bear hug, Mommy!" he says, throwing his arms around my neck and squeezing as hard as he can. I squeeze back and we laugh and laugh. "I did it for us," I tell him, knowing he can't possibly understand what I'm talking about. But he feels my love, the strength of the bear hugs, and we laugh again, rocking back and forth . . .

T wo months after the abortion I'm still sure I made the right decision. But sometimes, in the dark of the night, I wake up crying. Or in the middle of my everyday life a feeling of sadness washes over me. I've started going with Tiffany to those meetings for girls. I think it helps.

In September I'll enroll at Hamilton Heights City College. Ethan will go with me and stay at the day care center on campus on the days I have classes. Things are working out. I wish I hadn't been so stupid, but I can't change the past. Right now, I'm working on the present and the future. For Ethan. And for me.

Beyond Dreams

*I live two lives—an American life at school,
and a Vietnamese life at home.*

1

In my dream it is nighttime, darker than black, yet I can see. I am very small. My mother is holding me so tight I can't breathe. Her face is fierce. We are rocking, rocking. Screaming voices, thundering ocean, howling wind. Breathe! I want to breathe! Men stand over us, pull at us. I awaken, shaking, gulping air, my voice caught in my throat. I am afraid to go back to sleep, to hear what I'll hear and see beyond the darkness to what I don't want to see. I lie with my eyes open, pulling myself out of the dream, into tranquil thoughts of blue skies with white clouds, of birds in flight, of cleansing rain and warming sun.

Although it is not yet light out, I get up from bed, go to my desk and switch on my study lamp. My history book is still open to chapter 12, and I begin studying the pros and cons of the Marshall Plan. It will keep me from the darkness of my dream, and make the A I hope to get on Friday's test more of a certainty.

With the first rays of sunlight the dream sinks back to the dark place, the place where it hides, waiting to catch me in some unguarded moment of sleep.

Khanh, my twenty-nine-year-old brother, looks disappointed when he comes to my room and sees me already up and at my desk. I think he takes a mean pleasure from waking me up on school days, poking me in the arm and yelling at me, "Wake up, you lazy!"

I like being up, taking away his excuse to poke and yell at me. After I finish rereading chapter 12, I shower and dress, drink a glass of juice, and pick up the lunch money my mom set out for me before she went to work.

On my way to school, about a block from Hamilton High, I hear a familiar voice booming behind me, "Hey, Twinkie!"

I know without looking that it's Leticia.

"Hey, Oreo," I yell, turning back toward her, laughing.

We've been best friends since fifth grade and that's what we've always called each other. One of our other friends is Candice. We call her White Girl. When we go anywhere together, Candice always walks in the middle, like the filling in an Oreo, or a Twinkie. It's a joke that's become a habit. Our Peer Counseling teacher, Ms. Woods (Woodsy for short), says these names are racist, but I don't think so. I think racism is in the heart, and I know our hearts are good.

I watch as Leticia runs past a bunch of slow-moving kids, stretching out her coffee brown, track star legs, and catches up to me.

"Hey, Girl. I tried to call you last night. I thought it was grocery shopping night for your guards."

"It was, but Khanh got off work early, so they were back home by the time you called."

"I *hate* how King Khanh hangs up on me with that 'not home' business!"

"I know. The only ones I'm supposed to talk to on the phone are Jenny and Linda, and then I've got a five-minute limit."

"Man, that's flat out prejudiced. Just because I'm black, and they're from Vietnam and I'm *not*, he hangs up on me."

"Well, he hangs up on Candice, too."

"Don't you get tired of that mess? I sure wouldn't let my brother censor my phone calls. No, sir! He better not even *think* it."

"It's different in my family, though. When my mom's not

around, or busy, what Khanh says goes."

"It'd go straight down the toilet in my house!"

Even though Leticia and I are really good friends, there are some things about me she doesn't understand, like how I live two lives—an American life at school, and a Vietnamese life at home. Like at school my name is Tammy, and at home it's Trinh. It's the same for Jenny and Linda. They have different names for school than the ones their parents gave them when they were born. And they can hardly ever talk on the phone, or go out, either. Their families put a lot of pressure on them to excel in school, just like my family does.

"Remember what your mother said when you wanted to drop Honors English because it was so much work?" I say.

"Yeah. She said it was up to me. I should do what I thought was right."

"That's what I mean. I can't even *imagine* what it would be like to hear those words coming from my mom or my brother. I don't think Jenny and Linda's families ever tell them to do what they think is best, either. First, our parents know best, then our aunts and uncles know best. Then our older brothers know best. That's just how it is."

Leticia says, "No way would I let my brother tell me what to do—my mom, though, that's a different story." Leticia laughs. I have to laugh, too. Leticia's mom is *big*. Nobody crosses her.

My mom is only about five feet tall, and she probably doesn't weigh more than a hundred pounds, but size has nothing to do with who's the boss. There's a Vietnamese saying, "Children sit where their parents place them." And in my family, I'm still a child.

My dad died on our way to this country, when I was only three. So that made Khanh the man of the family, even though he was just fifteen at the time. It's strange. Sometimes I miss my dad, even though I don't remember him. How is that possible?

I have no memory of anything before kindergarten. From something my auntie said, I know I was very sick on the first boat trip, before we got to the Philippines. And once, when I was still really young, I heard her say something about pirates, but my mom shushed her. I wonder if the dream that lurks in the darkness and comes without warning, always the same, started in my life before memory.

Whenever I ask my mom about that time, or about how my father died, her face goes all hard looking, and she says, "Yesterday's gone. Don't reach into deep waters or you may become food for sharks."

She tells me to honor my father's memory, but she offers nothing to help me remember. All I know of him is how he looks in a faded picture that sets on a shelf dedicated to deceased family members. And I know he smoked Camels because my mother puts a pack of Camels beside his picture every year during Tet.

I wish my mother would help me remember my father, and understand my past, but it's not her way. Even so, I know she made huge sacrifices to get us to this country, and no matter how closed and hard her face sets, I will always love and respect her for what she's done. Jenny and Linda and I talk about this sometimes. We all feel the same way. Our parents risked everything to give us a chance in life, and we will always honor them.

On the way to my locker, after lunch, I get caught in the middle of some guys who are horsing around in the hall. It is too crowded. I freeze, my hands over my face, trying to breathe. Frantically, I push through the mob and stand leaning against my locker, trying to free myself of the nightmare fear that has invaded my daytime life.

"Let's go," Leticia says, as she bangs her locker door shut. "Hey, what's wrong? You look like you've just seen a ghost or something."

I pull myself back to reality and take my calculus book from my locker. Leticia and I walk together to Peer Counseling. We take seats next to each other near the door. The desks are arranged in a sort of sloppy semi-circle, instead of in rows like in all my other classes.

I like this class a lot. We talk about everything in here—drugs, sex, family stuff, friendship, suicide, gangs, conflicts, goals—everything. What with my honors classes—English, biology, history, and French—plus calculus, not to mention Vietnamese school on Saturdays, Peer Counseling is like a picnic to me.

This is the first semester of my senior year. I thought your senior year was supposed to be easier, less pressured, but that's not the way it's working for me. I spend from five to six hours a day studying. And not just because my mother and brother insist on it either. No way could I keep up in my classes if I didn't study a lot.

When I was younger, school was fun for me. But since high school, it's felt more like I'm caught in a trap. Peer Counseling, though—that's like an hour where I can run free.

Woodsy sits with the rest of us in the large semi-circle of desks instead of sitting at the teacher/authority place in front of the room.

One of the requirements for this class is that we each do a project that relates to Peer Counseling. Leticia and I still haven't chosen a project. We want to work together but so far we can't agree on a subject.

Leticia wants us to sign up for the Safe Sex project. I'm *sure* I don't want to do that. I get so embarrassed just buying things for my time of the month I can hardly stand it. I can't see me standing in front of a bunch of ninth graders showing them condoms and diaphragms and all that stuff. Nothing embarrasses Leticia—she could do it easily. Me? I'd probably faint if I had to touch a condom. I'm all distracted right now just thinking about those things. My mom and brother would go crazy if they thought I knew *anything* about any of that. I do know, but not from experience.

Today is Josh's turn to report on his project, which is about dreams—not my favorite subject, especially after the dream I had early this morning.

"Has anyone ever dreamt they were falling?" Josh asks.

Everyone starts talking at once, about falling, waking just before they hit ground, or dreaming they're falling and actually falling out of bed, falling from cliffs, tall buildings, bridges, and on and on.

"Josh . . . " Ms. Woods says, standing. "Can you get some order in here, or should I reach for my whip?" She laughs.

Woodsy is tall, taller than Leticia, and skinny, with short, curly hair. She's very forgetful about little stuff, so she wears her glasses attached to one of those necklace things and her keys on a bracelet. But she doesn't forget the important stuff—like Leticia and I haven't signed up for a project yet.

I don't know how old Woodsy is—I can never tell. Some adults who I think are ancient turn out to be about thirty, and some who I think are only about twenty-five turn out to be fifty. Maybe she's forty-six, like my mom. Woodsy's not prejudiced like some of the white teachers around here. And she cares about students, not just about grades and test scores.

"Josh," Ms. Woods says again.

"I know, I know. Hey, everybody, one at a time, remember?" he yells over the noise. "It's as important to listen as it is to talk," he says, reading from a poster-sized list of communication skills that's tacked to the back wall, next to a giant red and white sign that says **No Put Downs!**

Listening is the easiest communication skill for me. I'd much *rather* listen than talk, except with one or two friends at a time. Then I can be talkative.

When things finally quiet down, Josh says, "I chose this topic because I liked the mystery of it—that a dream is a message from the unconscious, but the message is delivered in code."

"I heard that if you die in a dream, you're really dead. Is that true?" Tony asks.

"How could anyone ever prove that?" says my friend Leticia, always the skeptic. "That's stupid!"

"Leticia," Ms. Woods says, pointing to the **No Put Downs!** sign.

"Oops, sorry, Tony. I didn't mean *you* were stupid, I meant it was a stupid idea."

Everyone laughs.

"Hey, Twinkie, tell Josh about that dream you always have. You know, your fresh-off-the-boat FOB dream."

"No, Oreo Girl," I say, trying to make light of it. I don't even want to think about that dream, much less talk about it. I can't believe I ever told Leticia. I wish I hadn't.

Woodsy turns toward us, redfaced. "This is a no-put-down classroom, and I expect you all to respect that!"

I'm so surprised by Woodsy's anger that I just sit there, looking dumb, I'm sure. But Leticia says, "We weren't putting anyone down. How were we putting anyone down?"

Woodsy takes a few deep breaths, as if she's getting ready for an underwater swim. She glances at Josh.

"Josh, would you mind finishing up tomorrow?"

"No problem," Josh says, smiling with relief.

"I know we've done a lot with the concept of 'no put downs.' But it's not something you learn once and never have to think about again. Every one of us, including myself, slips up, either in anger, or ignorance, or for the sake of a laugh. But that doesn't mean it's okay."

It's not unusual for Woodsy to change the class schedule because of something that comes up spontaneously. But it's never been because of anything I've said or done. Right now I'd like to slide along the floor, under the crack in the door, and go be a worm in the weeds. Right now, I wish Woodsy *was* one of those teachers who only cares about test scores.

"What are some put downs you hear around school?" is the first question she asks.

Zach says, "Mr. Horton, in math, is always telling us stuff like 'pretend you've got a brain,' or 'pretend you're smarter than you are.'"

Tony laughs.

"Is that funny to you?" Woodsy asks Zach.

"Well, sort of. But it also makes me feel stupid."

"What else do you hear?" she asks.

Woodsy stands at the board writing words that kids call out: Retard, airhead, butthead, asshole, nigger, bitch, dick, low-life, stupid, slut, ho, FOB, chink, nip, wannabe, oreo, twinkie, honky, gangsta, yo mama, faggot, dyke, butch, player, lazy, loser, and on and on. Seeing all of those words on the board like that is amazing—knowing they are just a few of the ways people can insult each other and make each other feel bad.

Christy says, "But a lot of people just say those things as a joke. What's wrong with that?"

That gets the class going on what's really funny and what's just a cover for being mean and nasty. How do we feel, underneath it all, when someone calls us a name, trying to be funny? Does it hurt even though we laugh?

Woodsy asks, "Is it possible that even when used with humor, certain words such as faggot, or nigger, or chink, or FOB strengthen stereotypes that get in the way of our seeing each other as real people?"

I look at the clock. Ten minutes to go before the bell rings. I know this is the question Woodsy has been leading up to.

"Let's take the terms Oreo and Twinkie. Isn't that really saying a person is rejecting a big part of themselves, is two-faced and hypocritical?"

Tony says, "I think friends like to call each other names because it shows they're friends. Like I can say something to John that he'd smack someone else for, but because we're friends, we laugh."

"Have you ever seen that backfire?" Woodsy asks. "Someone gets hurt, or angry, when the other person thought they were just being funny?"

Several kids start talking about friends getting mad at friends. Woodsy listens and nods, then says, "Leticia and Tammy, I don't want to embarrass you. I know neither of you wants to hurt anyone. I don't want to put you on the spot just because earlier this period you said some things without thinking. We all do that. But . . ."

The whole class says, "**BUT . . .**" which reminds me that Leticia and I are not the only ones Woodsy has ever used to make a point.

"Yes, **BUT**. . ." Woodsy says. We all laugh, including Woodsy, and I'm no longer quite so embarrassed.

"When we call someone an oreo, or a twinkie, we're saying they're one color on the outside, and a different color on the inside. We're saying they have no respect for their heritage. Leticia, do you really wish you were white?"

"Nah, I know black is beautiful. Even Mattel knows that now. Toys-Я-Us has a whole section of African American Barbies."

"Tammy, how about you? Do you consider yourself yellow on the outside and white on the inside?"

"No," I say, thinking of the illustrations in my biology book, the crimson red of the heart, the blue of the veins. "It's just a joke."

"It's not so funny," she says. "And that FOB business . . ."

"But some people really are fresh off the boat," Tony says.

"Most are fresh off the airplane," Woodsy says. "Besides, it's another stereotype. Right? What do people mean when they talk about FOBs?"

"Stay off the road when they're driving," Tony says, laughing.

"They smell fishy," Mary says.

"Listen to me," Woodsy says. "When we talk about people who are new to our country as FOBs, or say they're all diseased, or on welfare, or a menace on the highway, or whatever gets said about such people, we're denying their individuality—their personhood. Unless we are pure Native Americans, somewhere along the line our families came from somewhere else."

"But I think some of that stuff is true," John says.

"Right," Woodsy says. "Some people who are new to this country *do* have T.B., or trouble learning to drive, or need public assistance for a while. And some are healthy and rich and excellent drivers. I want you to think about this. Is such talk part of the solution, or is it part of the problem?"

The bell rings at exactly the same time she finishes her statement and I'm out of there. Leticia and I walk together toward the gym, two among thousands trying to make our way to the next place.

"Old Woodsy was really on the rag today, wasn't she?" Leticia says.

"Yeah, I guess so."

"Hey, Twinkie," I hear a voice beside me. It is Candice.

"Hey, Girl," Leticia says. I notice she doesn't say White Girl, the way she usually does. I also notice that Twinkie doesn't sound as funny as it would have an hour ago.

"What's up?" Leticia says.

"Wanna do something Friday night? I'm available," she says, looking at Leticia. She knows *I'm* not available. The most my mom and Khanh ever think I should do is go to the mall on a Saturday. Even then I have to be home by eight o'clock at night.

"What about Donald?" Leticia asks.

"He's working late. He's trying to save enough money to rent a limousine for the prom."

"Hey, that reminds me of a dream I had last night," Leticia says. "Do you think that's true about dreams being messages? I had this dream that Albert came to get me in a big white limo, but when I went to get in, the door was locked. And then it took off flying, like an airplane. What kind of mixed-up message is that, anyway?" She laughs.

"Maybe you should tell that one tomorrow, when Josh gives the rest of the presentation, and leave me alone about my dream," I say.

"Hey, lighten up," she says. "I was only joking."

"So funny I forgot to laugh," I say.

"Man, everyone's losing their sense of humor around here. First Woodsy, now you."

"I've never had a sense of humor about that dream," I say.

Leticia looks at me for a long time. "Yeah, I guess I knew that. Sorry," she says.

Leticia and I almost never get mad at each other, and when we do, it's over fast.

2

Late in the afternoon Jenny calls and my Mom hands the phone to me. "Five minutes," she says.

"Tammy, what did you write about on that Marshall Plan question in history?" Jenny asks.

I get my papers and we talk about the history assignment. Then I ask, "Jenny, do you think Twinkie is a racist term?"

"You mean like when people call *you* Twinkie?"

"Yes, or anyone."

"Well, I think if someone called me Twinkie it would be racist because I don't like it. But I think it's not racist for you because you like it."

"Ms. Woods says it's always racist."

"Well, I can understand that, I guess. Like maybe it means there's something bad about being Asian through and through?"

"I don't know," I say. "I'm not sure I get it."

We talk a little more about history, then Mom yells at me, "Time's up," and I hang up.

I take the world map I've been working on into the kitchen and spread it out on the table. The map has borders from 1945. Things used to be very different than they are now. This is the last major history thing I have to do before finals. I've been working on it for two weeks. It looks good—neat, with distinct colors. I just hope it's accurate. Some of that information was hard to find.

My mom is standing at the counter, still in her white nurse's uniform, cutting meat into tiny segments and stir frying it with vegetables and seasonings. We'll eat that with our rice. I watch her for a minute. She doesn't smile much, but when she's preparing food she has a slight, almost unnoticeable smile around the edges of her mouth. I used to like to help her in the kitchen. She taught me to make some dishes *her* mother used to make. Sometimes, around Tet, I help with food preparation. But mostly all I do at home is study.

Mom's kind of a quiet person, unless she's mad—then she yells at me—she and Khanh both. I hate that yelling. Leticia's mom talks polite to her, and so does Candice's. When I told my mom once about how nice their moms were to them she got that hard, closed look on her face and said those women should be ashamed to be raising such lazy daughters.

I can feel Mom looking at me now. It's weird. Even though we don't talk much, she seems to know when I'm thinking about her. I continue coloring Australia. She wipes her hands on the dish towel and walks over to the table. Pointing to Vietnam, she begins talking about her country, my country, the country of our ancestors. I don't think her country is my country. I don't even remember Vietnam. And the country she remembers is way different now, so who even knows Vietnam? It doesn't seem real to me, to think of Vietnam as my country. I will vote in the next election, so maybe the United States is my country. But that doesn't exactly feel real to me either.

Khanh comes in and sits at the table opposite where I'm working on my map. My mom brings him a bowl of rice and the meat mixture and places chopsticks on the table. He thanks her in Vietnamese, in the formal respectful way that English cannot accommodate. English is more direct, straight to the point.

We never use English at home. My mother is afraid we will forget our Vietnamese language if we don't use it together. Also, speaking English would turn things upside down, because I am most fluent in English, then Khanh. My mother just knows the basics for her job as a vocational nurse.

Sometimes I try to use English with Khanh, in the car, before we get home to our Vietnamese lives. But he refuses to listen if I speak to him in English. He says it is disrespectful—too informal a way to address the man of the household. I don't think that. I think straightforward English puts families on a more equal level. But equality within our family is definitely not what Khanh wants. So, as the saying goes, I sit where I am placed.

Just as Mom fills her bowl with rice and starts to sit down at the table, the phone rings and she picks it up. There is a very long silence, then she begins talking loudly, first fast, then more slowly. I stop my map work and look up, alerted by the intensity of her voice. Khanh, too, has stopped eating and is sitting very still, listening.

"Khanh!" She motions to him, waving paper and pencil.

"Write it down!" she says. "Write it down!"

Khanh takes the tablet and pencil from her as she thrusts the phone toward him. She turns toward me, tears dampening the broadest smile I've ever seen on her face. "What is it?" I ask.

She puts her arms around me, laughing and crying at the same time. "Lan. Your cousin from Saigon, Auntie Trang's daughter. She will be here soon."

My mother goes back and forth, reading what Khanh is writing, patting him on the shoulder, patting me. I have never seen her look so happy.

"How I miss my sister, Trang. How I miss Trang. And now her daughter will be with us. For certain Trang must soon follow."

Khanh hangs up and tells us that this coming Saturday, at four-twenty in the afternoon, my cousin's flight will arrive at LAX. Mom grabs the phone and calls Auntie Mai, telling her the news, her voice and manner filled with excitement.

"They got a good airfare, so they took it for Lan," Mom is saying.

"What about her parents?" I ask.

"Her father is not well enough to travel, and Trang must stay to care for him. But Lan must get started in school here. Already it is late."

"How old is she?"

"Sixteen."

"Why didn't they come here when the rest of our family did?" I ask.

She only shrugs. Even such a simple question about my time before memory must go unanswered. I roll up the map and take it into my bedroom, then sit at the desk and open my English literature book. From my window I have a good view of the house across the street. The two kids who live there are only in junior high, but I see that already they have more freedom than I do— coming and going at all hours of the day and night, yelling smart answers back to their parents. When I'm alone, just being me, I sometimes wonder how my life would be if I were one of those kids, or if I were Leticia, or Candice.

Also I wonder what my life will be like next year, in college. I'm going to Cal State Fullerton. Khanh is buying a new car and is going to give me his old one, so I can commute. It's cheaper than living on campus. But even though I'll still be living at home, I know I'll have much more freedom as a college student than I do now.

I hope Leticia will go there, too. She's been accepted, if she can just get the financial stuff together. She may end up getting a track scholarship, then she wouldn't have to worry about money.

Khanh has everything worked out for me—some financial aid, some scholarship money, and some help from him. He's good at figuring things out. I'll say that for him. And he's worked hard. He just graduated from college two years ago, at twenty-seven, because he's had to work full-time days and go to school at night. My mom works, too, but she doesn't make enough to support us all. I guess Khanh's a good person. He's so harsh sometimes, though, that I forget he cares. But he wouldn't have worked all the college plans out for me if he didn't care. Except maybe he cares more for his idea of me than for the real me. And who is the real me? Maybe it *has* been a mistake to be that joke-Twinkie girl. I honestly don't know.

Tonight, as I look out my window, I wonder about my cousin. Will she look like me? Will she be nice? Will she want to hang around me all the time? Will she dress like a typical FOB? Will she help with the housework?

Just as I've stopped daydreaming and started to get serious about my English assignment, I hear my Auntie Mai and Uncle Hoi's voices at the front door.

"Come in, come in," my mother calls to them. There is a lot of laughter and excited talk, but I stay at my desk and try to concentrate on my homework.

It is after ten o'clock when Auntie Mai comes into my room and sits on my bed. When I was younger and we all lived in the same house I was really close to Auntie Mai. She was playful—not so serious as my mom, and she always made me laugh. We've not been so close the last few years, though. I'm not sure why.

"This is very happy news, Trinh," my aunt says.

I turn my chair around so I sit facing my aunt. "I guess," I say. "I don't even really know her."

"Oh, but she's your cousin. You'll love her."

"What's she like?"

"I don't know, really. She was only two when we left. She was a very sweet baby. And her mother, Trang, is the sweetest of all the sisters, so Lan's probably still sweet. It will be a big Tet celebration this year," Auntie Mai says, smiling.

She reaches into her pocket and pulls out a Reese's chocolate peanut butter cup and hands it to me.

"Thank you, Auntie Mai," I say with a smile. For as long as I can remember, my aunt has always had something in her pocket for me.

For the first time ever I don't want to go to Peer Counseling. First, I'm embarrassed about yesterday. And second, which may really be number one, I don't want to hear about dreams.

"How about someone's after you and you can't run, or you're

trying to scream and nothing comes out?" Mary says.

"I don't know," Josh says. "In the books I used for this report they kept saying everyone has to figure out their own dreams, but if it's a dream you keep having over and over again, it's an important message and you should pay attention to it."

"What if you want to stop having a dream that you have a lot?" I ask.

"I think that's one of those things you're supposed to pay attention to," Josh says.

"But what if it's scary? I mean *really* scary?" I ask, thinking of how I wake up from my unwelcome dream, shaking and unable to breathe.

"Right," Tony says. "I hate that—someone's trying to kill me, and I can't run or yell or anything."

"Well . . . " Josh says, shuffling through some papers, looking confused.

Woodsy says, "I want to back you up on the importance of thinking about dreams and reflecting on our inner workings, Josh. It's a way to more fully understand ourselves. Without self-understanding you go around doing things and not even knowing why. *That* can get you in trouble. It's important to probe beneath the surface, look beyond your dreams to the messages they have for your life."

That seems like the opposite of what my mom always advises—don't reach into deep waters. Who's right, I wonder.

"I dream about the boogeyman," Mary says.

Lots of people laugh, but Woodsy says, "Make friends with the boogeyman. He's part of you. Make friends with the dark side of yourself."

Tony hums the Twilight Zone tune and we *all* laugh, including Woodsy.

At the end of the period, when Ms. Woods passes the project clipboard, I see that almost everyone is signed up for something. But there's still a big blank opposite my name. Leticia's, too. Besides us, the only other blank spaces are next to Roger, Marcus, and Tony—three of the biggest do-nothings at Hamilton

High. We've got to come up with a project—soon.

"Maybe we should sign up for the Safe Sex project after all," Leticia says.

"Filled," Ms. Woods says. I'm relieved.

"How about tutoring in a beginning English as a Second Language class?" Ms. Woods says. "We still need more people for that project."

"I don't know," I say, handing back the clipboard.

"You speak Vietnamese, don't you, Tammy?"

I nod my head.

"You could be a great help in an ESL class. They desperately need more people who can talk with kids who are new to this country and haven't learned English yet."

I sit looking down at my notebook, saying nothing. I don't know why, but I don't want to have anything to do with those classes, or with the kids who go there. Like I said earlier, I don't speak Vietnamese at school and I don't speak English at home. I don't want to mix things up.

When I don't respond, Woodsy says "Well, find something. It can be almost anything as long as it centers on a common problem and offers some possible solutions."

"We will, Woodsy. We'll sign up tomorrow for sure," Leticia promises.

Later, Leticia says, "We've got to get a project, Girl."

"Maybe we should volunteer at Manor Retirement Home," I suggest. "Michelle says she likes that. She's reading to one of the ladies who can't see well enough to read anymore."

"I can't do that. It's too depressing. It's bad enough I've got to go see my grandma in one of those places. It's sad. Remember how she used to always be laughing and cooking, always telling some story while we hung out in the kitchen?"

I laugh, remembering how when we graduated from junior high school Leticia's grandmother helped us throw a party.

"She makes the best biscuits in the world."

"Made. She *made* the best biscuits in the world. She's not making anything now, sitting in a chair, mumbling stuff nobody can understand."

"We'd be at a different place than your grandmother is," I say.

"Yeah. Different but the same. They all reek. You do it if you want, but I've got all the retirement home visits I can handle . . . How about just signing up for tutoring and getting it over with?"

"No way. The FOBs over in those classes make me nervous. Nothing against them, but I'd rather not be around them."

"You were fresh off the boat once," Leticia says.

"Don't remind me," I say. For an instant I get that outsider, stand-quiet-by-the-wall feeling I had in kindergarten, before I learned English. Before I learned to be like everyone else. I close those old feelings out.

"My cousin from Vietnam is coming here on Friday," I say.

"To visit?"

"No. To stay."

"Just her? No mom or dad?"

"Her dad's sick. As soon as he gets better they'll come, too."

"She staying with you?"

"Yeah."

"An FOB in your very own house is okay, but you can't bring yourself to tutor in the ESL classes? You're crazy, Girl."

"I suppose you're the picture of sanity? Like you're afraid to go to a retirement place and read to some little old lady?"

Leticia laughs and crosses her eyes at me.

"Maybe we'll have to work on different projects—you in ESL and me at the retirement home," I tell her.

"Maybe. But I'd still rather come up with something together. Woodsy said we could find our own project."

"But what?"

"Maybe it will come to us in a dream, like Josh says happens with inventors sometimes."

"I don't like dreams," I say.

"All the more proof you're crazy. I love dreams. It's like a free movie in my own cozy little theatre."

"There's nothing cozy about my dreams," I say.

3

Saturday morning as I'm getting ready for Vietnamese school, Mom comes into my room. She is dressed in red, for luck.

"No mall today," she says.

"But, Mom . . . " Her face hardens and I only *think* what I want to say. Saturday afternoon is my only time to be free. She agreed that as long as I'm getting all As, I can go to the mall on Saturdays with my friends. What that means is, after Vietnamese school in the morning, I come home and help clean house, and then, around three or so, I can go to the mall. I look forward to Saturday afternoons all week long.

"Your cousin arrives today. We must meet her."

"But there will be lots of people to meet her," I say.

"No one her age but you," my mother says.

And that is that. I go with my brother and mother to meet Lan. Auntie Mai, Uncle Hoi, and my three cousins wait at our house, the women preparing food and the men watching TV, I suppose.

Khanh has made a big sign with Lan's name on it which he holds up as people begin pouring through the gates from flight 1721. My mother stands on tip-toe, straining to see over the crowd in front of us. I doubt that she will recognize Lan, based on the only picture we have of her, taken at the age of two.

When it seems there can be no one left on the plane, a timid-looking girl walks through the gate and sees Khanh's sign. Her face breaks into a smile and she moves toward us, hesitant.

My mother calls, "Lan! Lan!" and the girl nods yes.

"Auntie Le?"

My mother runs to embrace Lan, crying. Lan, too, is crying.

"Come, we'll get your luggage," Khanh says, gently taking Lan's arm. I can hardly believe she is sixteen. She looks more like about twelve, she's so thin and frail.

On the way home, in response to my mother's questions, she tells of her trip. First she flew from Saigon to Bangkok, then from Bangkok to Hong Kong. Her plane was late arriving in Hong Kong, so she missed her connection. Finally she got another flight out of Hong Kong to Hawaii and from there to Los Angeles. It's been over twenty-eight hours since she left home.

I flew to San Francisco once, with Auntie Mai. That took about an hour.

"Twenty-eight hours?" I say, not certain I've heard correctly.

"Better than ten months," Khanh says, surprising me with a reference to the silent subject of our trip out of Vietnam.

When we get home, Auntie Mai has food waiting for us. There is a meat and noodle soup, rice with fish sauce and vegetables, and sweet cakes. My mother introduces Lan to everyone, then carries her two suitcases into my room. As she sets them on my bed, I get a hint of the changes that are about to occur in my life. Where did I think she was going to sleep, anyway?

In the dining room, Aunty Mai stands behind Lan, rubbing her back. They are talking about Lan's mother and father.

"How much we miss our sister," Auntie Mai says, "and how happy we are to have her only daughter with us."

"And your father?" Uncle Hoi asks.

Lan shrugs her shoulders. "About the same," she says.

I sneak a look at Lan. I wonder what it's like to have a father—even one who's been sick much of her life. I put bowls and chopsticks on the big table and Auntie Mai calls the men to come eat. After they are seated and everything is on the table, Auntie Mai pours tea for everyone and the rest of us sit down. The talk is lively, and I see that even though Lan is quiet, she has somehow brought energy to the rest of the family. Except me. I don't feel so lively because I've lost my Saturday at the mall.

When the phone rings, Khanh picks it up. "No talk now," he says, and slams down the receiver. Anger rises within me. I *hate* that he controls my telephone calls. And I hate that he's so rude to my friends. It's not fair!

I sit picking at my food. I really wanted pizza tonight. That's what I'd be munching out on if I were with my friends.

Lan is eating like she's starved, telling my mom how much she likes the soup, how it tastes exactly the way her mom's does. My mom is beaming at Lan. Usually at dinner Mom is always urging me to eat more of whatever she's cooked. Sometimes it seems like an obsession with her. But tonight she doesn't even notice that I'm not eating much.

After dinner Lan shows the pictures she's brought with her, and answers over and over again that she doesn't know for sure when her parents will come to the United States, but it will be as soon as her father is well enough to travel.

Uncle Hoi asks, "Does Hung still run the factory? How much do eggs cost? Is old Doctor Phu still alive?" Question after question which she answers in her soft voice, the rhythms of her Vietnamese speech untouched by America. I listen longer than I expected to, then say good-night to everyone.

"Lan must be very tired now. We will have time for more questions tomorrow," my mother says, taking Lan by the hand and leading her to my room. Mom helps Lan unpack, making space in my chest of drawers for Lan's things. She hangs up two dresses, one skirt, and two blouses, and a traditional *aó dài* dress, then kisses us both on the cheek.

"You're lucky to be like sisters now," she says as she leaves the room.

I get pajamas from my drawer and take them into the bathroom to change and brush my teeth. When I come back, Lan is sitting on the bed in a thin white nightgown. Her clothes are folded carefully on top of the chest of drawers. I crawl into my bed and scrunch up on the far side, next to the wall. Lan scrunches up on the other side.

"Goodnight, Cousin," she says.

"Goodnight, Lan."

Even though Lan and I are not touching, I feel crowded in my bed. And I feel cheated out of a precious Saturday. I concentrate very hard on not dreaming as I drift off to sleep.

Monday morning Khanh takes us to school. Khanh *never* has time to take *me* to school, but now that Lan is here he suddenly has time. Lan is wearing a light-weight dress that comes to below her knees. It is dark grey and has long sleeves. She looks as FOB as they come.

Even my mother, who is not at all style conscious, told Lan this morning that we'd better get her some more clothes soon. I've been asking for money for weeks for this great pair of pants I saw at J. Crew, but now it's Lan who's going to get new clothes.

"Come with us to the office," Khanh tells me. "I'll get her started enrolling, then you wait with her and walk her to class when she gets her program."

"Khanh! Bancroft has a fit if anyone comes in late."

"You wait until she's finished and walk with her to class. And meet her after school and ride the bus with her," Khanh says, in a tone that allows no argument. So I stay until Lan is officially enrolled, and then I walk with her to the orientation center where she will be tested and then placed in "appropriate" classes.

It is already 8:30 by the time Lan is settled. No use going to first period and risking Ms. Bancroft's anger. The trouble is, she won't take my homework if it's late, so besides a cut she'll drop my homework grade. All because my brother insists I babysit for Lan. If I lose my A in that class, it will be all his fault. But he won't see it that way.

During lunch Leticia and I go see Mr. Wong and get set up with a tutoring schedule. Because I am fluent in Vietnamese, I am assigned to a class for the very beginning Asian students. Leticia, because she's taken Spanish, is assigned to a class that's mostly Hispanic kids. We'll be tutoring during our lunch period, on Tuesdays and Thursdays for six weeks.

Instead of meeting Leticia and Candice after school and hanging out with them until the bus comes, I have to go to Lan's last class and wait for her to be finished. I stand outside the door, looking in at the thirty-five or so kids who have no idea if Twinkie is a put-down or a compliment, but then, I'm wondering about that myself.

Lan has a worksheet on her desk and seems to be deep in concentration. She is one of the last to leave her desk after the bell rings. I walk in to get her.

"Hello. Hi," she says, proud that she has learned a greeting.

"Hello," I say, smiling back.

Lan begins talking to me in Vietnamese, racing on about her classes, asking questions. I don't answer. It's not that I mean to be rude, but I've never spoken Vietnamese at school. It's like crossing a boundary or something. The words won't come from my mouth. It's not until we get to my front yard that I begin to respond to the questions she asked back at school. It's weird, I know, but that's how I am.

My mother greets us, her face open and not hard. Lan follows her to the kitchen and I go to my room, to sit at my desk and study, as I always do on school days. I open my calculus book and begin working through the day's problems. It is not until the last equation is finished that I notice the unfamiliar sounds of easy talk and laughter coming from the kitchen, mingled with the everyday sounds of food preparation.

In the week before Tet, Lan and Mom become more and more of a team in the kitchen, preparing elaborate dishes with ingredients that can only be found in a special Vietnamese market near downtown Los Angeles. Some of these, the special rice cakes that have to be wrapped in banana leaves and boiled for a day, are only for Tet. But a lot of the cooking gets eaten the day it's prepared. My mother gives Khanh a list before he goes to work in the mornings. They're always two days ahead in their planning, so they don't have to wait for Khanh to get home from work before they start in the kitchen. Auntie Mai and Uncle Hoi just happen to drop by at dinner time more often these days. My mother doesn't even ask me to help with the cooking anymore. Not that I want to, but it seems kind of strange to me that she doesn't even ask.

In bed one night, in the dark, Lan says, "Cooking with your mother helps me not miss my mother so much. That's something we always did together. And Auntie Le and my mother do things exactly the same way. It's funny. They hold a knife the same way, and they stir things with the same quick movements."

Lan laughs, but I think it is to keep from crying. For the first time I think how lonely it must be for her here. And I wonder what happened that I stopped cooking with my mother.

Just after midnight at the beginning of Tet, my mother comes into my bedroom and calls to Lan, "Get up. It is time."

I look up sleepily, wondering what's going on. My mother leads Lan out the back door and around to the front, being sure that Lan is the first to step through our doorway on this day.

"For luck," my mother says as Lan climbs back into bed.

Over the three days of Tet, we pay special attention to the memory of our ancestors, setting out favorite foods beside their pictures. (The only picture that gets cigarettes is my father's.) We dress in our traditional clothes and go to a big Tet festival at the Vietnamese Center. Lan and I get money from our family. Nothing is very different from last year, except somehow it seems that my family has become even more Vietnamese since Lan arrived.

At the Center I take good luck leaves from a special tree so I can put them under my pillow. I hope they will protect me from the dream of darkness.

CHAPTER

4

At school it turns out that I am assigned to tutor two new students in the ESL class. Lan is one of them. The other is a boy, Dat. They both ask about a million questions in Vietnamese, and I answer in English, drawing pictures to try to help them understand.

"Tell me in Vietnamese," Lan pleads, as I'm trying to get across the meaning of "today," as in "How are you today?"

Later, at home, I explain, in Vietnamese of course, that for me, school is only for English, home for Vietnamese. Except for Vietnamese School on Saturdays. At that school I only speak Vietnamese.

"I don't understand," Lan says.

"I don't either, exactly."

One day, just as I am going into the ESL class, Candice walks past me and yells, "Hey, Twinkie."

I wave and walk into the room where Dat and Lan are waiting for their tutoring session.

"What is Twinkie?" Lan asks.

Dat proudly pulls a Twinkie from his backpack.

"Twinkie," he says with a grin.

"But why are you Twinkie?" Lan says to me.

"Home," I tell her, meaning I will explain in Vietnamese when we get home today.

She shrugs and turns to Dat. "American ways are strange," she says.

Later, when I try to explain to her, yellow on the outside, white on the inside—a joke—my words sound hollow. Lan says to me what she often says when I try to enlighten her about my double life. "I don't understand."

A few days later, as I'm leaving the ESL room, I hear some boys in the hallway making jokes about FOBs.

"Don't breathe," one of them says as he gets near the door. "That's the T.B. ward in there."

Another one makes a fake, racking cough noise. I look back inside, at the kids who are trying so hard to learn English, who've come here with hope in their hearts, and I am suddenly very, very sad. And then I feel an anger rising hot within me, for them, and for me, and for all of the put downs people endure. And I suddenly know in my heart what the "No Put Down" sign in Peer Counseling really means.

When I see Leticia and Candice after school I say to them, "I don't want to be called Twinkie anymore."

"Are you taking all that stuff Woodsy says seriously?" Leticia says.

"I'm taking *me* seriously," I say.

"Okay," she says.

"I don't get it," Candice says.

"I'm just telling you, no more Twinkie for me. I'm more than a Twinkie. And I'm not calling you White Girl anymore, either. You're more than just a white girl."

They both look puzzled. We walk to the bus together, but no one says anything.

Saturday, over pizza, Leticia says, "I've been thinking."

"Whoa," Candice says with a laugh.

"No, really. The Twinkie stuff. I hate to lose a joke, but sometimes Oreo doesn't seem so funny anymore either."

"I don't care about White Girl," Candice says.

"Yeah, but that's not saying you're one thing on the outside and something else on the inside," Leticia says.

"But *I* think it's still a put down, because it says you're only a stereotype," I tell Candice.

"Maybe," she says, "But it doesn't bother me."

"Think about it," I say.

"No thinking today. It's Saturday."

"Let's go check out that new video place," Leticia says.

"Why? Are you mad at Albert again?" I ask.

"No, but it never hurts to look around," she says.

We wander down there, but it's filled with junior high boys.

"Man, where are the real guys?" Leticia says.

We go into a few shops, try on some clothes, check out Tower Records, get a frozen yogurt, and then it's time for me to meet Khanh out in front of Nordstrom's. My one afternoon of freedom is over until next week.

When I get to the spot where I always meet Khanh, it is Auntie Mai instead, who is waiting for me in her car. She smiles as I get in and hands me a peanut butter cup.

"Did you have fun?" she asks.

"I always have fun with Leticia and Candice," I say. "They make me laugh."

"Why don't you invite your cousin to join you next time? I think she needs to laugh, too."

I don't know what to say. Even though I see Lan at school, she is part of my home life, my Vietnamese life.

"I don't think she knows English well enough to get along with my friends," I say.

"She is learning fast," Auntie Mai says.

"I know," I say, thinking of how much more quickly she catches on to things than Dat does. I'm not sure if she's smarter, or if she studies more than he does, or what.

We ride along in silence for a while, then Auntie Mai says, "It is a lonely time when people first come to a strange new country. I know it was very difficult for Lan to leave her mother."

"Then why did she?" I ask. I don't plan for it to come out mean-sounding, but it does.

"She came for the same reason we all come," my aunt says. "To find a chance for a better life."

We ride the rest of the way home without talking. I feel a barrier between us, but I don't know how to get past it. I really don't want to start taking Lan to the mall with me on Saturdays. It would change everything.

When we pull into the driveway at my house, Auntie Mai stops the car and turns to me.

"What happened to my sweet little Trinh?" she asks, then answers her own question, "America."

Monday morning, as usual, Khanh comes in and pokes me in the arm, hard, and says in a mean voice, "Wake up, you lazy."

I sit straight up in bed and scream at him, "Don't poke me and don't call me lazy!"

He stands looking at me, stunned. Lan jumps out of bed and runs to the bathroom.

"You don't tell *me* what to do," he screams back at me.

"I'm tired of this," I tell him. "It's not necessary. I've got an alarm clock that can wake me up without hurting me, putting me down by calling me lazy."

"You don't tell *me* what to do," he says again. He takes a step closer and raises his arm. My mom appears in the doorway, watching. He turns and leaves. I breathe deeply, relieved, hardly believing that I stood up to him—well, really, I only *sat* up to him. That makes me laugh, all by myself, in my bedroom, sitting on my bed. I *sat* up to him. I wonder what will happen next.

"You scared me," Lan says on the way to school.

"Me, or Khanh?"

"*You* because you made him mad."

I want to say more to her, but we're out of the house, in the American part of my life, and it's too complicated for her to understand in English. Maybe we'll talk later, about why she says *I'm* the one who scared her, when it's Khanh who acts all tough.

The next morning I am surprised to be awakened by the alarm clock, not by Khanh. He doesn't speak to me for four days, but he also doesn't poke me and call me lazy anymore.

Some months after Lan has been here, the dream starts again. I awake, trembling. I don't care about all those ideas about how important it is to let your dreams tell you something. I don't want this dream! Lan turns on the light, concerned.

"It's nothing. Only a dream," I say, trying to discount the fear within me. "Go back to sleep."

She turns off the light and soon I hear the deep, regular rhythms of Lan's sleep. Me, I battle sleep, forcing myself to repeat in my head the list of presidents and the dates they held office, from George Washington to now. The arrangement of biological classification. "King Philip Come Out For God's Sake"—Kingdom, Phylum, Class, Order, Family, Genus, Species. The five kingdoms: Animalia, Plantae, Fungi, Protista, Monera—so many living things, how important is the dream of one *Homo Sapiens*?

I keep myself awake until dawn by pulling facts from my memory, repeating them in my mind, shuffling through them and then refiling them. As the sky grays on its way to dawn, I drift into the sleep my body craves but my soul fears.

In the morning I turn off my alarm and, finally, am overcome by sleep. Lan shakes me gently. "Get up you lazy," she says, mimicking Khanh, laughing. I drag myself out of bed, knowing all he needs to start his old poking and yelling routine again is for me to oversleep *one* morning. I jump in the shower, dress, and get to the breakfast table at my usual time.

"Good morning, Trinh. How are you this morning?" Lan asks in the formal beginning English dialogue she's memorized from her textbook.

"Fine," I answer in Vietnamese.

After school and dinner and cleanup, I stay up until one in the morning, studying, hoping if I am exhausted by the time I crawl into bed I will not dream. But it comes to me again, the huge waves against the boat, my mother holding me, her face fierce but frightened, and the men closing in around us, reaching for us, and I cry out, suddenly awake, my body stiffened, expecting blows.

"I sometimes dream of my father, too," Lan says.

I lie there, hovering at the edge of my dream, not understanding what Lan is saying.

"Your father," Lan says. "When your body trembles, just before you awaken, you call out to him."

This puzzles me, but I don't want to pursue it. It is bad enough that I have no privacy in my waking life. At least I would like to keep my sleeping life to myself.

"I am afraid I will never see my father alive again," Lan says in a sleepy voice. "But at least I have known him. I know this is very selfish of me, but I was relieved to leave home. I was afraid of seeing him die. I know he is dying. I miss my mother so much, but I live in hope that I will see her again. I think, though, I must have said good-bye to my poor father forever."

Lan must be almost asleep. She is rambling in a dreamy way. I am only half listening, longing for sleep and afraid of it, when she says, "I've been afraid of seeing my father die ever since I was very young, when my mother told me of how you, my cousin, had witnessed the death of your father."

My whole being awakens. I hold my breath, listening to the story I knew but didn't know, the story beyond the dream, as Lan continues her slow, captivating reverie.

"Always I was interested in my American cousins, because I had no more cousins in Vietnam. I would ask my mother to tell me stories of you and your brother and Auntie Mai's children and I would beg to come join you. She would only say, 'Soon.' When I would ask how soon, she would talk of other things."

I listen very carefully, waiting for her story to turn again to my father. I am afraid that if I ask, she will realize there are secrets, and she will close up, as my mother and brother used to close up when I was young enough to hope for answered questions.

Lan continues in her sleepy way, "One day when I kept pestering my mother about when we could come live near you, she said we had to wait until we could leave legally, not risk the dangers of trying to escape by boat. I cried, saying I wanted to see my cousins right then.

"That is when she told me of the pirates, and how they tied your brother to a railing at the front of the boat. Then, at the back, they beat your father to death in front of you and your mother.

"She told me your mother tried to cover your eyes, and one of the pirates took her hands from your face, so you could see it all, and of how your mother said your screams and hers must have followed your father all the way to heaven. And they were no more or less than the screams of many mothers and many children, who witnessed horrors too terrible to be remembered."

I am crying now, screaming as I must have when my mother's hands were pulled from my eyes. My mother and Khanh rush into the room, my mother reaching for me, pulling me into her arms, holding me in a fierce embrace. In my mind I see what I've not seen in my dream, my father, beaten lifeless, lying bloody and still before my three-year-old eyes, and I cry out to him as I must have cried out then.

My mother is now, as in my sleeping visions, crying, praying, rocking, holding me so tight I can barely breathe, and in the grip and the rocking I feel her protection. I feel her love.

"It is over, it is over," she chants. My sobs are uncontrollable, crazed. Khanh stands at the foot of the bed, his face drained of color. Lan is standing by the door, watching, trembling. Slowly the pain that must cry out subsides.

"It is over. It is over," my mother repeats.

I don't know if it is over or not, but in the depths of my darkness I see a dull light spreading. I understand now that I must seek my own light, and that my mother cannot help me reach beneath the surface. It is not that she doesn't care. It is that there are places she must not revisit.

"I'm all right," I tell her. "I am all right." We sit on the bed in silence, still touching. She reaches for Khanh, and he takes her hand.

"You couldn't help it," she says, and I know then the shame he must have felt, at fifteen, when he could not save his father. And I understand the desperate drive with which he struggles to keep me under control, protected from all of the real and imagined dangers of America.

I go to Lan, who is still standing stiff and scared in the doorway. I put my arms around her and whisper, first in Vietnamese and then in English, "Thank you, Cousin." The moment I say those words, I know I'm going to stop dividing my life into Vietnamese at home and American everywhere else. That has been the biggest put down of all, and I've done it to myself, by pretending to be some kind of Twinkie-girl joke. But I'm beginning to see what is right for me. All of the influences on my life are a part of me, American and Vietnamese, family and friends, good times and bad. Finally, I realize that I'm a person who must not fear dreams. I must reach below surfaces and look beyond dreams.

Uncle Tweetie

*Right now I feel like taking my sleeping bag and hibachi
and going to live in a cave in the foothills, in private.*

1

Aunt Vicky comes out with a tray of iced tea and cookies.
"I thought you boys could use a little cooling off about now,"
she says. "Josh?" She holds a glass out to me and I take it.

"Thanks, Vee," I say, using the nickname I've had for her
since before I could say Aunt Vicky. I set my hammer on the
sawhorse beside me. I'm dripping wet from the heat, and from
working so hard.

"It's coming along, isn't it?" she says, running her hand along
the new drywall seam, then handing the other glass of iced tea to
Rick, my brother.

"Great," Rick says, smiling. "We'll finish the walls today. I
guess it'll be another week or so before we're done with everything."

Rick is going to be living up here, in San Luis Obispo with our
aunt, so he can go to Cal Poly. My folks said they couldn't afford
to send Rick away to college, but when my aunt offered to let him
stay in a little room at the back of her property, my parents agreed
to let him go. That was good news for me. I've been trying to get
Rick out of my room ever since Dad moved him in about twelve
years ago. When my dad started his own business, he took over

one of our bedrooms for an office. Rick's a nice enough guy, I guess. But he thinks he can boss me around just because he's two years older than I am. And he's a slob. It'll be a relief not to have to smell his sweaty socks and T-shirts all the time. He has this habit of tossing everything into a corner until it practically rots and then, when my mom refuses to let him borrow her car until his laundry is caught up, he does a mammoth wash. So for about two days a month our room doesn't stink. But things will be different from now on.

When I leave here in a week or two, I'll go home to my own private room, with my own private stereo. My dad promised me a new stereo for all the work I'm doing up here on my aunt's place.

"I just can't believe the change in this place," Vee says, looking around the room.

It really was a mess when we first got here. Someone had lived in it a long time ago, before Vee moved into the front house. But nothing had been done to it for years. The ceiling tiles were all rotted out because of a leak in the roof. The floor tiles were messed up, too. Water had seeped into the walls, and if you leaned against the wrong spot, your hand would go right through the wall. We've been working steadily from morning to night since we got here a week ago, and it's beginning to show.

The first thing we did was check out the electrical connections and hook up Rick's stereo. Then we started making repairs. My dad does remodeling and we've been helping him on jobs for as long as I can remember. Sometimes it's a pain in the butt, going to a job on Saturday when my friends are off having fun, but at least I know how to fix stuff.

Sometimes in the late afternoon we take a break for a quick swim at Avila beach. Man, that is cold water compared to the beaches down south. And the waves are little, no challenge. But it's refreshing. After that, we go back to Vee's and work until dark.

"Have some more cookies," Vee says. "Keep your energy up."

I grab three more. I don't want to seem like a pig, but I could easily eat about two dozen of these things right now.

"When do you register for classes?" Vee asks Rick.

"I see an advisor the twelfth."

"I'm glad this is working out for you," she says.

"Me, too," Rick says. "It's really important to me to be able to go away to college. Thanks, Auntie Vee," he says, smiling the smile that some girls find charming.

"Hey, I'm getting plenty out of this deal besides the pleasure of your company. Having this room fixed up probably adds thousands of dollars to my property value."

"We're all happy," I say. "I finally get Rick out of my room."

"*Your* room?" Rick says.

"It is now," I laugh. "I can hardly wait to get back home—put my new posters up on the walls, get my own stereo set up, hear my own music. Not have to be hearing that old-timey jazz stuff that you always play."

"Yeah, now you can listen to Michael Jackson all the time," he says sarcastically. I swear, I liked Michael Jackson for about a week once, and Rick won't ever let me forget it.

"And you can listen to red-neck music," I say.

"Hey, watch it, Josh," Vee says. "Don't start insulting *my* music now. We may not be as sophisticated up here as you folks are down in Southern California, but we've got music with heart."

"You're just like Mom," I say, nodding at the ancient wreck of a Toyota parked in the driveway. "You put more money into Patsy Cline and Willie Nelson CDs than you do into your cars."

She laughs. "Your mom and I have to keep in touch with our roots, Josh."

The phone rings in Vee's house and she walks quickly out the door and across the yard. Rick and I get back to work. We've just one more drywall panel to install and that part of the job will be over. That's the hardest part. The floor tiles will be easy, then we'll paint, replace a broken window, and put on a new front door. I think that will be it.

It's nearly five now, and cooler. One thing I'll say for San Luis Obispo, the air is fresh, not all smoggy like at home. It feels good to take a deep breath and not feel like you're poisoning yourself just by breathing.

"This is going to be so cool," Rick says. "My own little pad. I think I'll get one of those futon things, and a couple of bright colored pillows. We should have about a hundred bucks left even after we buy paint."

I can't believe Rick the slob has his mind on interior decoration. I'm looking to see if maybe he's suffered some kind of heat stroke when I hear the creak of the screen door again.

"That was my cousin, Precious," Vee says. "Aunt Chickee died this morning."

At first I don't understand what she's talking about. The people next door have chickens. Did one of them die? But Vee looks like she's trying not to cry. This probably isn't about a chicken. I just stand there, looking at my hammer. I really hope she doesn't cry. I never know what to do when people cry.

"Aunt Chickee from Arkansas?" Rick says.

"Yes," she sighs. "I just feel so sorry for Uncle Tweetie. You remember them, don't you?" she asks, looking back and forth between me and Rick.

"You probably don't remember him," she says to me. "I think you were only about three when we all made that trip to Arkansas. But you probably remember some, don't you, Rick?"

"I remember getting car sick and throwing up on Josh," he says. God, I remember that too, now.

"Thanks for the reminder," I say, sarcastically.

Vee laughs. "We were in that old Dodge van of your dad's. No air conditioning, and you guys fought all the way across the state of Texas. That's probably the reason I decided never to have kids," she says.

We laugh again, and then she turns away. I guess she's crying, but I don't know if it's because of this Aunt Chickee person, or because she never had kids. She'd have been a really good mom. I don't think us fighting was the reason she didn't have kids. I think she knew her husband was a butthole, and she knew what a rotten father he'd be. She finally left him about ten years ago. That's when she moved up here.

"I told Precious I'd call your mom and let her know, too," Vee says, walking back toward the house.

Rick and I stand watching her for a minute, then turn back to our work.

"Maybe I do remember him," Rick says. "I think he's the one who let me sit on his lap and steer his car all the way into town one day. I liked him. And Aunt Chickee took me with her when she milked the cow. Man, that was creepy. I stopped drinking milk until we got back home to the stuff that came in cartons."

By seven o'clock we're finished taping the last piece of drywall. We go into the house to wash up.

"We're going to go get some pizza, Vee," I say. "Want some?"

She sighs. "No, thank you. I'm not very hungry right now."

"Did you call Mom?" Rick asks.

"Yes. She's worried about Tweetie, too. You know, when your mom and I were kids, after our dad died, Uncle Tweetie and Aunt Chickee used to have us spend summers with them. Uncle Tweetie was kind of like a second dad to us . . . he's eighty-seven years old, and he's all alone now."

At the restaurant, over pizza, we start laughing about the names of relatives on my mom's side of the family.

"What, is this the bird family or something? Tweetie and Chickee?" I laugh. "What's the name of that place where they live?"

"Flat Hill, Arkansas," Rick says, choking on his soda.

"They should live in Aviary, Arkansas," I say.

"There's that other guy mom told us about, too," Rick says. "Uncle . . ." he can't say it for laughing. "Uncle . . ." I don't even know what's so funny and I'm laughing so hard I can hardly catch my breath. Finally, Rick blurts out for the whole restaurant to hear, "GOOBER! UNCLE GOOBER!"

Now we've totally lost it. The waitress is watching us like

maybe we're dangerous. I can't help it.

"I think they named him after a peanut," Rick says.

"Or boogers," I say, prompting another loud burst of laughter from Rick.

When we get back home I go to Vee's house to shower. She's sitting at the kitchen table with a box of photos in front of her.

"Come look at this," she says, holding a photo out for me to see. "There's Uncle Tweetie and Aunt Chickee, and me and your mom in front. I think we were nine and ten there."

I peer intently at the two little girls, Vee and my mom, trying to see what remains of them in the grown-ups I know today.

"There's Uncle Goober and his boy, Taft Hartley, standing next to Tweetie . . . both of them are gone now, too," she says sadly.

I look through the pictures with her, listening to her stories.

"I don't know why they called her Chickee," she says. "Maybe because she was little and cute. She was strong, though. She could work circles around most of the men. But Tweetie, your great-grandma named him. Grandma's mother. You remember stories about her—our Grandma Tucker?"

I nod. I don't really remember stories about her, but I don't want to say that.

"Well," Vee says, "when Uncle Tweetie was born, his mama started calling him Sweetie, because she said he was the sweetest baby she'd ever had. That was saying something, because she'd already had twelve by the time he was born."

"Twelve? Twelve?" I ask, amazed.

"Right. Twelve," Vee says. "That's how they did things then. Anyway, pretty soon everyone was calling him Sweetie, except for your great-grandma Tucker, who was only two and couldn't say Sweetie. She called him Tweetie, and it stuck."

"So what's his real name?" I ask. "You know, like on his birth certificate."

Vee laughs. "From what I've heard, no one gave a thought to

birth certificates down in the country then. And by the time the last of the fifteen kids were born, the parents had run out of names, I guess. The later ones didn't even get named at birth—the parents just waited to see what people would call them, and their names sort of evolved—like Tweetie, and Goober."

"Where'd that one come from?"

"He was little, like a peanut."

"Weird," I say, but as I look at all those photos of people when they were young, and old, and in-between, I get this strange feeling, like I've got part of them in me. And I feel guilty for laughing at their names.

2

Two weeks later I'm on my way home, driving down Highway 101 in my dad's pick-up truck. I feel so free it's like I'm flying. I've never ever driven so far alone. The windows are down and the radio's on full blast. I can't find anything but country western but I don't even care. Life is cool.

First thing when I get home I'm going to go pick up my stereo. Then I'm going to put the posters that I got at the Cal Poly bookstore up on the wall in *my* bedroom. They're weird in the extreme—drawings by some old guy named Escher—full of optical illusions and misleading things—like you think a staircase is going to one place but when you look closely it's totally different. I don't even know why I like them so much. Just because they're weird, I guess.

Anyway, after I get my music set up, and my posters up, and spray a little pine scent in the room to get rid of any leftover Rick odors, I'll go across the street and invite Tracy to come listen to some music with me. Tracy is who I love, but she doesn't know it. No one knows it but me. We've been friends for a long time, but one day, just before school was out, I looked at her, and I looked again, that was it. I was in love.

Tomorrow morning I'll register for classes at Hamilton High School. This is going to be a cool year, my junior year—no more hearing Rick yell at me in the halls at school, "Hey, baby brother." And I'll get to use the car more often because Rick won't be around to be borrowing it.

I think I'll probably make varsity basketball this year. I've grown taller in the past six months, and I've beefed up some too, with all the construction work I've been doing. I don't feel so much like a kid anymore.

By the time I can get a decent rock station on the radio, the sun is covered with a gray haze and I'm tasting smog. I don't care. It'll be good to be home.

I pull into our driveway about six-thirty. In time for dinner, I hope. I grab my duffle bag and the carefully rolled Escher posters and get out of the truck. God, it feels good to stretch my legs. Mom and Dad come out to greet me.

"Hi, Josh. I've missed you," Mom says, giving me a big hug. Dad hugs me, too.

"Vee called a while ago. She said you boys did an excellent job on the room. I'm proud of you," Dad says.

"We have a surprise for you," Mom says.

Maybe they decided to get that weight set I've been wanting. We could take Rick's bed out and there'd be plenty of room. I hope that's what it is.

I've still got visions of a padded bench and weight rack when I see him sitting at the kitchen table—white-haired, skinny, wrinkled up like some old turkey neck. He's eating Cream of Wheat. I don't know much about fashion, but I'll bet his suit has been in and out of style three or four times since it was new.

"Uncle Tweetie," Mom says to me, like she's announcing the President of the United States. She's all beaming, like this must be the best news I've ever heard.

"Is this Josh?" he asks, standing and stretching his hand out to me. It's bony, and cold, but he's definitely got a grip. He can't be more than five feet tall, and he's got a broad nose and a wide smile that makes him look sort of like Happy in that Walt Disney movie about the seven dwarfs.

"Well, ain't you just as handsome as can be?" he says, still pumping my hand. "You could be a movie star I betcha. You ever go down to Hollywood where all them movie star people are?"

"Uh, no," I say.

"Well, it's close, ain't it?"

"It's about fifteen miles from here," Dad says.

"Ooooie," he says in a long drawn-out sound, "I didn't know it was *that* far away. I thought y'all were right close."

Mom laughs. "You've just flown over fifteen hundred miles, Uncle Tweetie."

"I know that's what they say, Sugar, but I cain't believe it."

I carry my stuff back into my room. There's a Bible setting on the bedstand between the two beds. I hope he doesn't turn out to be a religious fanatic. God, I wonder how long he's staying? I put my rolled-up posters in a corner of the closet. It doesn't seem like they'll fit here, with Uncle Tweetie.

Next to the Bible, on *my* table, is a can that once had creamed corn in it. What's *that* doing in here? I pick it up and check it out. It's got some nasty brown gunk in it. I carry it to the kitchen, throw it in the trash, and wash my hands.

"You got anything sweet, Baby?" Uncle Tweetie asks Mom as she picks up his cereal bowl and takes it to the sink.

"I got you a rhubarb pie," she says to him.

"Rhubarb? Y'all got rhubarb clear out here in California?"

Mom just laughs and gives him a peck on the cheek.

"Well, let me try some of it," he says, reaching into his back pocket and pulling something out.

I can hardly believe my eyes as I watch Uncle Tweetie slip his lower plate of false teeth into his mouth.

"Want a piece of pie?" Mom asks me.

"Is that the only kind you got? Rhubarb?"

She nods.

"No thanks."

"Why, I swear, this pie is about nearly as good as Chickee's rhubarb pie," Uncle Tweetie says to my mom. Then he makes a funny choking sound. Mom goes over to him and puts her arms around him while Dad pretends to be totally involved in TV.

"I know she's in a better place," he says, "but I miss her so much, all the time. Sixty-eight years I've been wakin' up to her purty face."

"I know," Mom says. "I know . . . You must be tired now. Why don't you go to bed, and we'll talk some more tomorrow."

He gets up and walks to the sink, rinses his lower plate, and puts it back in his pocket. Gross. I watch Mom leading him to my room, *my* room. So much for the first thing I'm going to do when I get home is set up my stereo. I flop down on the couch in front of the TV.

"How was your time with Vee?" Dad says.

"Okay," I say. I really don't feel like talking.

"I thought we'd run over to Circuit City and get the stereo set-up I promised you."

"Nah," I say.

"What do you mean 'nah'? You've been dying to get your own stereo and now you're saying 'nah'?"

"I'll just wait until Uncle Tweetie leaves," I say. "I mean, he's going to bed at seven o'clock. It's not like I'd have a place to listen to music."

"Well, get one with headphones," Dad says.

"It's not the same, Dad," I say.

"Well, I won't beg. Let me know when you're ready."

Mom comes back into the kitchen and starts rummaging around, moving papers and dishes.

"Lose something?" Dad asks.

"Uncle Tweetie can't find his spit can. Have you seen it?"

"Not since he got here," Dad says. "I thought he left it in the bedroom."

"Spit can?" I ask. "What do you mean, spit can?"

"Well, it's Uncle Tweetie's," Mom says. "It's what he spits his dip of snuff into when he's finished with it."

"You mean that creamed corn can?" I ask, feeling my stomach rise.

"Yes. Have you seen it?"

"I threw it away. God, Mom, it was rank."

"Well, I'll just have to find another can for him," she says.

She opens a can of tomatoes, empties the contents into a plastic dish, rinses the can, and takes it back to what I'd recently been thinking of as my bedroom.

"That makes me want to puke," I say to Dad.

"Well, you know, Josh, he has different ways than we do. He's just a country old-timer."

All I can think of is the gunk in the creamed corn can that looked like something you'd find in the oil pan of some wreck of a car.

"Come on, Josh," Dad says. "I know how you feel about your room, but he's old and he needs some help. You're hardly ever home, anyway. Don't over react."

That's what my dad always says when I'm about to get screwed—I know how you feel and don't over react. God, he doesn't have a clue. Right now I feel like taking my sleeping bag and hibachi and going to live in a cave in the foothills, in private.

"How long is Uncle Tweetie going to stay?" I ask.

"I don't know," Mom says. "As long as he needs to. He helped me and Vicky out a long time ago, when we needed help. Now it's our turn to help him."

"Why didn't he go to Vee's then? She's got as much room as we do now that the back house is fixed up."

"Because he came here. That's all. And we'll all make him welcome, Josh . . . You'll like Uncle Tweetie. You'll see."

Right. My mom thinking I'll like someone is a good sign of the absolute opposite. Like the time she set me up with her friend's daughter. "You'll really like her," she'd said.

This girl didn't have a date to some big dance, which should have told me something from the beginning. But my mom told me it was because she, Penny was her name, went to an all-girls school and so she didn't have a chance to meet any guys. I swear,

I don't know how I let myself get talked into stuff, but I do. Besides, my mom said she'd buy me *three* new CDs, and she'd let me borrow the car either Friday or Saturday of the next four weekends. I guess you could say I took a bribe.

When I went to pick Penny up for the arranged date, just as I was leaving, Mom said, "Remember, it's the inner person that counts." Man, I should have never left the house that night.

Then there was the time my mom was being Mother Teresa or somebody. She had this kid in class, Isaac, who lived just with an older brother and was like totally unsupervised. Mom teaches English at Margaret Sanger Junior High, near downtown. Anyway, she decided what this thirteen-year-old wannabe gang banger needed was a role model. "You'll like him," she'd said. "You just have to get to know him." So she brought him home after school one day and I taught him how to play backgammon and shot a few baskets with him out in our driveway, and after she took him home I was missing twenty dollars and two CDs. So to hear my mom say I'm going to like Uncle Tweetie does not make me feel great about Uncle Tweetie.

I go out to the garage, get the basketball, and start shooting baskets. Under my breath I mutter every cuss word I've ever heard, the "F" word, the "M-F" word, the "C" word, and all the little ones like shit and crap and bastard. I've about come around to the "M-F" word again when I feel Mom's hand on my shoulder. I shut up.

"Josh, why are you so angry?"

I shoot another basket.

"Josh."

I don't look at her. I stand bouncing the ball.

"Josh, Honey, Uncle Tweetie may not even be here very long. Don't be mad about something that may not even be a problem. Okay?"

"But, Mom, it's like I don't have any say at all. Every other guy I know has his own room, a place to have friends over, to play music. I've been waiting sixteen years for my own room! Then you and Dad just decide you'll move some old man into *my* room without even bothering to talk to me about it."

"Be reasonable, Josh. You weren't even home, and it all happened so fast . . ."

"But you didn't even care about how that would be for me!"

"We do care, Josh. But we care about Uncle Tweetie, too."

"More than your own son?"

"Of course not, Josh. Now you're being extreme."

"Why isn't he sleeping in *your* room? You're the one who invited him. Or how about the bedroom Dad calls his office—put him in there." I shoot another basket. It's stupid to try to talk to her. She'll never get it.

"You know, Josh, there's more to life than having your own room."

I shoot another basket. She stands and watches me for a while, then turns and goes inside.

I throw the ball hard against the backstop, back up, catch it, throw it again. I stay out there until the next door neighbor calls out his door, "Eleven o'clock!"

That's all he ever says to anyone—eleven o'clock. When we first put up the backstop and hoop we had to agree not to play past eleven o'clock. I think he's got his alarm set. I slam the ball against the garage door, twice, then go inside. My first evening home was not at all what I planned. No new posters up, no new stereo, no listening to music with Tracy in my room—just this old shriveled-up old Tweetie-bird in the bed across from mine.

3

In my dream I'm with Tracy in a forest. She's holding my hand and smiling at me. We hear a funny sound, like an animal that's hurt. Then we see a box of kittens, like you see sometimes outside a market, with a sign saying "Free to good home." Tracy picks up a kitten and hands it to me, but it keeps mewing and mewing, and then she's gone and the kittens are gone but I keep hearing the mewing. I turn over and know I've been dreaming, but the sound from my dream is still there. Through my window I can see the beginning of the grey light of early morning. I glance at my clock. Five-twenty. God. I listen, only half awake.

" . . . all our sins and griefs to bear. We should never be discouraged, take it to the Lord in prayer."

It is Uncle Tweetie, lying flat on his back in Rick's bed, singing.

"Uncle Tweetie," I say, ready to tell him I don't like to have to wake up before my alarm goes off at seven, but he starts talking.

"Mornin', Son," he says. "The Lord gave us another day." He smiles a toothless smile.

I see that his teeth, both uppers and lowers, are sitting on the table between us, next to the can Mom gave him to replace the one I threw away. I turn over, hoping to go back to sleep.

"Me and Chickee met at a singin' at a church over in Arkadelphia," he says, in the kind of mushy way people without teeth talk.

"Every mornin' when we woke up, and every night before we went to sleep, we sang a song. Sang together ever' Sunday down at the Free Will Baptist Church, too. I don't reckon we coulda lived together without that regular singin'. We both have strong opinions," he says, as if she were still alive. "I been meanin' to ask you, Son. You been saved? I don't see no Bible in this room but mine."

I stick my head under the pillow and will myself back to sleep.

The smell of coffee, bacon, and fried eggs fills the kitchen. Mom, Dad and Uncle Tweetie are sitting there munching out.

"Is it Sunday?" I ask, thinking maybe I've got my days mixed up and can go back to bed.

"Wednesday, Josh," my dad says. "I'll fry you an egg as soon as I finish eating," he says.

"Okay," I say. I don't know why we're having a real breakfast when it isn't even Sunday, but I'm happy to eat it. Maybe they're trying to impress the old guy. I look over at him, peppering his egg. He has his teeth in now.

"How is Cleopatra doing?" Mom asks.

"She's the same, Baby. You know, she was out hanging up her washin' one day and she just fell outta the world. I don't think she's ever comin' back."

"But she's still living by herself, isn't she?"

"Conrad brings her food, and they have someone go in and clean twice a week in the mornings. I reckon she's as well off there as anywhere."

Mom asks about Conrad then, and Precious and Henry and about a hundred people I've never heard of. Usually it's rushed at our house in the mornings but I guess Mom and Dad must have gotten up earlier than usual. Maybe Uncle Tweetie sang *them* awake this morning, too.

As I leave for school, Dad is trying to teach Uncle Tweetie how to use the remote control for the TV.

I'm halfway down the block when I hear Tracy calling me.

"Josh. Wait up."

I turn to see her in white shorts and a top that shows part of her stomach. Her hair is sunbleached and she's got a great tan. I think about how she held my hand in the dream and I feel my face and neck getting all hot. I hate that! I hope she doesn't notice.

"Walk with me," she says. "Are you on your way to register?"

"Yeah. I have a nine o'clock appointment."

"Me, too," she says.

We walk the seven blocks together, talking about our summers. She's been at her dad's most of the summer, someplace down near San Diego. I want to tell her how great she looks, but the words get stuck in my mouth.

"What classes will you be taking?" she asks me.

"You know, the usual college prep stuff. And Peer Counseling. I want to take that. My brother liked it a lot. He says Mrs. Woods is a cool teacher."

"I've been thinking about that, too," Tracy says. "But I want to take ceramics, too. I can't fit two electives into my program."

"Take Peer Counseling," I say. "It'll be fun."

"Which period are you signing up for?"

"Fifth. It's either that or second, but I'd rather take it in the afternoon. Get the boring stuff over with in the morning."

"Maybe I'll do that, too."

God, will she really change her plans to take a class with me? Is it possible she might secretly love me, the way I secretly love her? I doubt it, but there she is, smiling at me like she at least really likes me.

After I get signed up for classes I go down to Barb 'n Edie's with Brian. He's a really good friend, but he's been away most of the summer, too. We get caught up, and I eat my way through a garbage burger. I love those things. There was no place in San Luis Obispo that had anything like it. We hang out for a while, stop by McDonald's, where our friend Jason works, but he's busy, so we leave. Brian tells me all about how things are going with him and Danielle, but I don't tell him my hopes for Tracy.

"It's time you got a woman in your life," he says.

"I'm working on it."

"Who?" he asks, but I won't say.

When I get home late in the afternoon, the TV is blasting out, louder than I would ever play my stereo, if I had a stereo, and a place to play it. The house is empty. I turn off the TV and start looking around. Maybe Mom got off school early and took Uncle Tweetie somewhere. I get myself a Coke and a bag of potato chips and go outside to shoot a few baskets. That's when I see him, sitting on the ground in his overalls, staring up into the big walnut tree that grows in our backyard.

"What're you doing?" I ask.

"Well, Son, the danged TV was too loud, and no matter what I did, I couldn't change it. So I left."

"How long have you been out here?"

"Since I tried to find that program about the other side, and it got so loud I couldn't stand it."

"Well, I've turned it off. You want to go inside now?"

"I reckon. I get a little stiff sittin' on the ground for a very long time. But you've got you a coupla big old squirrels up there," he says, pointing into the tree. Then he turns and gets on his hands and knees, crawls to the trunk of the tree, and grabs onto it to help himself up.

"I don't get around so good anymore," he says. "I got the Arthur Ritis."

He brushes off his hands and knees and starts walking toward the house.

"You know, son, we'd get us a pretty good stew outta those two fox squirrels. Get me your gun and I'll get us some dinner."

At first I think he's kidding, but then he says, "My eyes ain't as good as they used to be, but I can still shoot me a squirrel. And those things in your tree don't even have sense enough to run away. I already told 'em they was dinner, and they just sat there. Arkansas squirrels are smarter than these California squirrels, but I reckon these'll taste just as good." He laughs a high-pitched laugh that, no matter how much I don't like sharing a room with him, makes me smile.

"Go on, Son, get me your gun."

"I don't have a gun," I say.

He gives me a long, slow look, tipping his head back to look me in the eye. Then he shakes his head slowly, back and forth.

"Don't have a gun?"

I shake my head.

"Ooooie, we *must* be comin' into the last days if a boy like you ain't even got somethin' to shoot a squirrel with." He looks me square in the eye, then turns slightly away and spits a big glob of that crankcase stuff in the dirt.

"Well, then, bring me your daddy's gun," he says. "Them squirrels are gonna get tired of waitin'."

"Dad doesn't have a gun, either," I say.

"Lordy, Lordy, this is about the sorriest mess I've been in," he says. "Squirrels just waitin' to be dinner, and me without a gun."

Uncle Tweetie shuffles dejectedly back to the house while I start banging away with my basketball.

When I go inside, about an hour later, Uncle Tweetie is sitting on the couch, staring out the window.

"It ain't your fault," he tells me as I walk past him.

"What isn't?"

"That you cain't shoot a squirrel," he says.

"I don't *want* to shoot any squirrels," I tell him.

"Well . . . that ain't your fault, either," he says. "Besides, a handsome movie star boy like you, I guess you don't need to shoot dinner even if it *is* right under your nose," he laughs. Honestly, he *does* look a lot like that Happy dwarf, except Uncle Tweetie's not as chubby. And I don't think Happy spits gunk into a can.

"I'm not a movie star boy," I tell him.

"Well, you could be. You was cute when you was little, too.

I'd crawl around with you on my back and you'd laugh 'til you got the hiccups. You used to laugh all the time."

"I don't remember," I say.

He nods, watching the tree again.

"Do you want me to turn the TV on for you? I can show you how to fix it so it won't be too loud."

"No, thank you, Son. I'll sit here with Chickee for a while. We always talk a little near sundown. Sing in the mornin', talk at day's end, and sing at night. All these years I been doin' that, I ain't fixin' to stop now. She's somewhere listenin' to me, I know that sure's I know the sun rises in the east and sets in the west."

"Okay, then. I'll be back after awhile."

I walk across the street, take three deep breaths, and knock on Tracy's front door.

"Hi, Josh, come on in," she says, flashing a smile that makes me think she's glad to see me. I follow her into the house. Photos are spread all over the coffee table and couch, and on the floor.

"I told Mom I'd put our pictures in albums before school starts. I didn't know I was talking about millions of photos," she laughs. "Look," she says. "This is when we were a family together, before my mom kicked my dad out."

There's Tracy's mom, dad, and older sister. Tracy is about four. They're all smiling and happy. That's the thing with pictures. Everybody looks happy, whether they are or not. Or maybe, for an instant when the picture is being taken, everyone *gets* happy. I think of the photos Vee got out when she first heard of Aunt Chickee's death. I guess that's why we take pictures— to remind us of happy times after people are gone from our lives.

"Look at this," she says.

It's a picture of me in the driveway, getting ready to shoot a basket. It looks like it was taken a year or so ago. I didn't even know she took it. I look at her, puzzled.

"I wanted a picture of you, and I was too shy to ask," she says.

I know I'm blushing. I can tell. And my face isn't the only place where there's an increased blood flow.

4

The second week of class Mrs. Woods hands out question-naires as part of an expanded understanding project we're starting. So far, Peer Counseling is my favorite class of the day, mainly because I sit next to Tracy, but also because the teacher is cool and it's more kick-back than any of my other classes.

"We'll look at racism, sexism, ageism, anything that treats people unfairly, or judges people unfairly."

We're supposed to get answers from at least two people in each decade, from pre-school to sixties. If we get one over seventy, we get ten extra credit points. If we get one over eighty, we get twenty extra credit points. Finally, a use for Uncle Tweetie besides the human alarm clock trick he does every morning at sunrise.

This morning, about five-ten, I was awakened by him sing-ing, "Never grow old, never grow old, In the land where we'll never grow old . . ." The funny thing was, he sounded almost young when he was singing it. Then he said, "Chickee, Sugar, watch for me. I don't reckon it'll be too much longer."

I'm not in any hurry for him to die. I wouldn't admit this to my mom or dad, but I've even started to like Uncle Tweetie a little.

He's a funny old guy, and he's always cheerful. But I sure would like my room to myself.

"Is it okay if we interview some of the same people?" Tracy asks Ms. Woods.

"Well . . . I don't want all thirty of you interviewing the same seventy-year-old, just for extra credit . . . How about if we say no more than two students can interview the same person?"

"Good," Tracy says, then turns to me. "Can I interview your uncle?"

"Sure," I say, all cool. But I wonder if she'll start thinking I'm weird because I have a weird uncle. We walk home together after school and I go into her house with her, like I've been doing every day since school started. Her mom doesn't get home from work until about six-thirty and her sister lives with the dad, so we have the house to ourselves. Yesterday I brought a bunch of my CDs over, so now we've got good sounds. We go into her bedroom and I start the new Pearl Jam. We sit on the floor, leaning up against her bed, listening for awhile.

Then Tracy says, "Come on. We can interview each other and get one of the teen decade out of the way." She takes the Peer Counseling questions from her notebook and asks, "Earliest memory?"

"Rick throwing up on me in the car."

"Yuck."

"How about you?"

"My dad banging on the door and yelling for us to let him in after my mom changed the locks," she says, looking away. "You're lucky that way. I bet your parents never even argue."

"Not much," I admit.

"Favorite childhood game?"

"Tether ball," she says. "But I was good at jump rope, too."

"Skateboarding. Does that count as a game?"

"Why not? If you could change one thing about the world, what would it be?"

"I'd do away with all homelessness," I say.

"I'd do away with all violence," she says . . . "If you could change one thing about your personal life?"

"I'd have my own room," I say. Then I add, "and I'd know for sure that you were my girlfriend."

Now it's Tracy's turn to blush. It's like the world is standing still, just for an instant, then she says, "I'd know for sure that you were my boyfriend."

I pull her close to me and kiss her on the lips. "I am for sure your boyfriend," I say.

"I am for sure your girlfriend," she tells me.

I kiss her again. It is kind of awkward, like our lips are at an angle or something. I've kissed girls at parties, but no one I've ever cared about very much. When we stop kissing I keep my arm around her.

"Did you mean what you said?" she asks.

"Yes. Did you?"

"Yes."

"I've wanted you to be my girlfriend for a long time," I confess.

"I've wanted that since before I took that picture of you," she says.

I guess, right now, I'm as happy as I've ever been. I start kissing her again, but then she pushes me away. But in an easy way, not like she doesn't like me.

"Let's go ask your uncle these questions," she says.

"I'd rather stay here and kiss you," I tell her.

"My mom'll freak if she comes home and finds us kissing. It's okay for you to be here if we're just friends, but if she even thinks we're holding hands she'll go ballistic."

Uncle Tweetie is on the couch, staring out the window when we get there. I forgot about it being his time with Aunt Chickee.

"Shhhh," I say to Tracy. "Let's go back outside for a few minutes."

She follows me out and we sit on the back steps. "Why can't we talk to him?"

"We'll go inside in a few minutes. He's talking with his dead wife now."

She looks at me like I'm totally crazy.

"Well, it's hard to explain," I say. "You'll just have to meet him."

She keeps giving me this strange look.

"You won't stop liking me just because I have a weird uncle, will you?"

She laughs. "I'm going to like you for a long time. I already have."

I tell her the story about how Uncle Tweetie got his name, and how he sings to Aunt Chickee when he first wakes up and just before he goes to sleep.

"I think that's sweet," she says.

"Yeah, well maybe he could come share *your* room then."

We go back inside and I introduce Tracy to Uncle Tweetie.

"Ooooie, you're a purty girl. You're one a them movie star kinds, too. When're you gettin' married?"

"We're only sixteen," I say.

"Well, that's not too late. Chickee was sixteen when we was married. You find a purty girl like this'n and you better grab her before she gets her cap set for someone else."

Tracy laughs. "Listen, Uncle Tweetie—is it okay to call you Uncle Tweetie?"

"Yep, cause you're gonna be part of my family real soon. I can feel it in my bones."

"Uncle Tweetie, we've got this questionnaire thing that you can help us out with. It's for school."

We explain the whole thing to him.

"Sure, I'll answer questions. I ain't got nothin' better to do. Unless—you got a gun, Tracy?" he asks, looking out toward the walnut tree.

"No."

"Well, then, I ain't got nothin' better to do."

We're still asking him questions, writing as fast as we can, when Mom and Dad come in from work, loaded with groceries and papers.

"Hi, Tracy," Mom says. "I haven't seen you around much. How are you?"

"I'm fine, Mrs. Finley. I've been away all summer."

"Well, we're all back in the swing of things now, aren't we?" my mom says, pointing to a stack of tests she's just put on the table. She's always grading papers, or making up lessons, or calling students.

My dad goes to the phone to call out for Chinese food. That's what we do once a week, on grocery shopping nights.

"Would you like to stay for a bite to eat with us, Tracy?" he asks.

"Well . . ."

"C'mon. It's really good stuff we get," I tell her.

"Okay," she says, "I'll call and leave a message for my mom, so she'll know where I am."

After she makes the call, we get back to the questions for Uncle Tweetie. When we get to the one about what he'd change about his personal life, he says, "I'd be with my Chickee."

Most of his answers go on and on, one thing leading to another. He tells us of his grandfather, who fought in the civil war, and of his grandmother, who threw boiling water on a Yankee who was trying to get into their smokehouse. I can't believe the stuff he's got in his head.

"I'd be on the Yankee side," I say. "There should never have been such a thing as slavery."

"Well, Son, if you was on the Yankee side, your great-great-great-grandma woulda threw boiling water on you, unless she'd had a gun handy. But that's war. It's all a sorry mess. I was too young for the Great War and too old for number two. Fine with me. I'm a farmer. I want to see things grow, not make 'em die."

He tried to explain his favorite childhood game to us, something called Snap. But we never got it.

He told us about how he'd been saved and how they'd baptized him in the river, next to a water moccasin, and it never even looked at them.

"You been saved?" he asks Tracy.

"Not that I know of," she says.

"You'd know it, Sister," he says. Then he shakes his head sadly, "I worry about you younguns, not bein' saved, livin' here where you get them big earthquakes, and not havin' sense enough to get married when anyone can see you been bit hard by that old love bug."

"Just two more questions," I say, eager to change the subject.

Those answers take another hour. It is eleven by the time Tracy leaves and Uncle Tweetie goes to bed. I think because he's stayed up so late he may sleep past dawn tomorrow.

No luck. At the first light of day he's singing, "I will meet you in the morning by the bright riverside, where our troubles will all pass away . . ."

He must know about a million songs. I bury my head under the pillow, but it's not enough to keep him out. "You'll know me, in the morning, by the smile on my face," he sings. Then he starts talking to Chickee. I finally drift back to sleep after he gets up.

Saturday morning, when I'm doing some clean-up stuff on the job site, Dad comes over to me with a soda.

"Want to take a short break?" he asks.

"Sure," I say, reaching for the can, wiping the sweat out of my eyes.

"I thought I'd offer you the stereo again," he says. "I'm glad to see you're liking Uncle Tweetie. He's a good man. I hope you're not still mad about the situation."

I don't know what to say. I *am* still mad at them, for the way they handled it. Liking or not liking Uncle Tweetie has nothing to do with it.

"I'd still like my own room," I say.

"So you don't want the stereo now, even with headphones?"

"Not until I have my own space for it," I say.

"Don't cut off your nose to spite your face," Dad says, and walks back to where the carpenter is working. I don't even know what he means by that.

The truth is, I'm at Tracy's house a lot more than I am my own now. Her mom is hardly ever home. Last night she called Tracy from work and said she had a chance to go to Laughlin with some friends for the weekend. Would Tracy mind? So she's going to be away until Sunday afternoon. Cool.

After we get back from the movies, I go home and check in. Tracy's kind of afraid to stay alone in her house all night, so I wait until my mom and dad go to bed. Then I go into my bedroom and lump pillows under the covers so it looks like someone is sleeping there, if no one looks too closely. Uncle Tweetie is sound asleep.

I could have just told my parents I was staying at Tracy's, but what if they'd said no? Better not to bring it up.

I tiptoe to the chest of drawers, reach into the back corner of the bottom drawer, and take one of the condoms Rick left behind. Then I sneak quietly out the front door and go over to Tracy's. I have plans.

We are stretched out on the floor, lying close to each other, listening to Boyz II Men sing about love. The only light in the room comes from a streetlight, filtered through drapes. I have my hand under Tracy's sweater, feeling the warmth and smoothness of her skin, below her bra. I move my hand up, to feel her breast. She moves my hand back down where it was. I kiss her, long.

"I can't get enough of you," I say. "I love you so much—I want to be with you in a way I've never been with anyone else." I look into her eyes, searching for the answer I want to see.

"Oh, Josh. I love you so much it scares me."

"Don't be scared. Don't be scared. I'll watch out for you," I say, kissing her again, moving closer, holding her tight to me. "Look," I say, reaching into my pocket and pulling out the foil-wrapped condom. "It'll be okay. I love you," I whisper, moving my hand up, slightly, closer to the place I'm longing to touch.

"Josh," she says, moving away from me, letting a space come between us. "I'm not ready. I'm sorry. I love you, but . . ." She is crying now.

"Hey, what's wrong?" God, I hate when people cry. I put my hand up to her face and feel her tears. What am I supposed to do now?

"I don't want to lose you. I'm just not ready, you know? When I am ready, I want it to be you."

"God. I'm ready," I say.

"I know," she says, resting her head on my shoulder. "And I really want to make you happy. And I want to be closer to you, as close as I can get. But I've thought and thought about it, and it just isn't time for me yet."

I sigh and put the condom back in my pocket.

"You probably won't love me anymore, will you?" she says, getting all teary-eyed again.

"I can't imagine not loving you," I tell her. "I think I might love you even more, if I could be with you in that way. But I can wait."

With this she starts crying again. I mean sobs, like a kid. "I was so afraid I'd lose you."

I hold her close and listen to the music as she gradually stops crying. I am about to burst with wanting her, but when it happens I want it to be right for both of us. And like they say in the Safe Sex talks at school, nobody ever died of an unsatisfied hard-on.

"Go get us some sodas, will you?" I whisper to her. "Let's watch TV for a while." I turn the stereo off, turn on this improv comedy show. These guys are really funny, and pretty soon Tracy and I are both laughing so hard we can hardly talk. I stay until about three in the morning.

"Call me if you get scared," I say.

"I'm fine," she says. She gives me the world's sweetest kiss, and I leave.

I think Uncle Tweetie is asleep when I sneak back into my room, but just as I pull the covers up over me he says, "You been with that Tracy girl?"

"Yes," I say. "She was afraid to stay alone, so I stayed with her for awhile."

"You oughta have your tail jerked in a knot," he says.

"Why?" I don't even know what that means, but it can't be nice.

"Because if'n you don't marry her, she's gonna get away from you, and then where'll you be? Soon as I fell for Chickee, I married her. Smartest thing I ever did, and I've done some pretty smart things in my time. Don't think I haven't."

"I'm too young to get married," I say, turning on my side, away from him.

"Hogwash," he says. "If'n you're too young for marriage, you're too young to be lettin' your bull loose in her pasture."

"My bull's not loose in her pasture," I laugh. "He's still in the pen."

"Thank the Lord. Me'n Chickee been piecin' on that ever since I woke up and saw you was gone. We both know no good comes from a quick romp in the pasture. Now a union blessed by God, that's somethin' that'll last you forever, not wear out by the end of spring."

"Didn't you ever, you know, want to . . . you know, let your bull loose before you and Chickee were married?" God, I can't believe he's got me talking this way.

"OOOIE, Son. I was on *fire* from the time I was twelve—on the farm, seein' the animals and the crops live their natural lives and I had to keep ever'thing all held in. OOOIE, I know that ain't easy. But it's kindly like the difference between the easy way, plowin' shallow and gettin' a puny crop, or plowin' deep and true, and gettin' a plentiful crop, livin' in abundance through the whole winter, with plenty left to sell . . . You asleep?"

"Almost."

"Sometimes I don't know when to stop talkin'."

"No, it's okay. I like your stories," I say.

"Well, good night, Son. I expect it's close to daylight."

"Good night, Uncle Tweetie," I say, turning on my side and letting my mind drift back across the street to Tracy.

I hear Uncle Tweetie say, "Good night, Chickee."

I swear, I practically say goodnight to Chickee, too. I've heard

Uncle Tweetie talk to her so much she's beginning to seem real to me. I wonder if I could get Dad to let me partition off part of the garage and put my bed out there? I asked him once and he said no, but if he hears me starting to talk to dead women, maybe he'll change his mind.

The truth is, though, old Uncle Tweetie has sort of grown on me. I'm still not wild about sharing my room with a spit can, or being awakened at dawn, every day, seven days a week, but I can't help liking him. And he and Chickee have given me plenty to think about.

Just before Thanksgiving holiday I come dragging in from school, loaded down with the books I need to get caught up on my homework. I toss my backpack on the bed, then go to the kitchen for a snack. Uncle Tweetie is sitting in the living room with his suitcase and his snuff can beside him.

"What's going on?" I say.

"Well, Son, I've got to be going home soon. I'm going to spend a few days with Vee and then get back to where I belong."

"But how will you get along, alone?"

"I'll be fine," he says. "Does it look to you like I cain't take care of myself?"

"No," I say, looking at his wrinkled, wiry old body and his broad smiling face.

"I'm more worried about what'll become of you. I hoped at least I'd get to see you be saved or married while I was here, but you ain't got sense enough to do either one," he says.

"When did you decide to leave?" I ask, thinking again how nobody ever tells me anything.

"Just this morning. I called and got me a bus ticket for San Luis Obispo. Vee said she'd carry me into some other San place in a few days and I can fly to Shreveport from there."

"San Francisco?"

"Nope."

"San Jose?"

"Maybe."

"But why don't you just visit Vee and come back? Why are you going home?" I ask, forgetting for a minute that this is good news and it means I get my room to myself.

"I'm sure the Lord knows everything. If His eye is on the sparrow, He *must* know I'm in California. But I just cain't help bein' afraid He won't know where to find me when he comes to take me to Chickee."

I don't know what to say to that.

Later in the evening, as he's leaving, he hugs me tight. "I love you and I'm prayin' you'll get saved," he says. "And if you don't marry that Tracy girl right soon, you ain't got the sense of a plowed-out mule."

I laugh and hug him back. After he leaves I spend some time thinking about how it would be, if I were a farmer, and Tracy and I got married right away. And how it would be to be so certain about God and heaven and being saved. But that's his life, not my life. I'm actually glad, though, that I got to know some things about his life.

I get out the Escher prints and tack them up on the wall. I clean the snuff dribbles off the table where his snuff can set. Then I start reading stereo ads. I'll go to Circuit City tomorrow. And there's a song I heard the other day that I think might help Tracy think it's time for us to be together. I mean, *really* together. It's not that I don't respect her decision to wait. I do. But every now and then I remind her of how much I want her, and how nice it could be, just in case she's ready to change her mind. And she reminds me of Uncle Tweetie's advice, not to take the easy way, but to work on something that will last, that will be abundant.

In the morning, I wake up with the sun, and it's almost like I can hear Uncle Tweetie singing, "When the roll is called up yonder I'll be there." And I know my mom was right when she said there are more important things in life than having your own room. But I may not admit to her that she was right for a long, long time.

ABOUT
THE AUTHOR

Marilyn Reynolds is the author of three young adult novels, *Too Soon for Jeff, Detour for Emmy, and Telling.* In *Too Soon for Jeff,* Jeff is a senior at Hamilton High School, a nationally ranked debater, and reluctant father of Christy Calderon's unborn baby. *Detour for Emmy,* the story of a 15-year-old who becomes pregnant, "vividly portrays teenage love and its consequences," according to *Publishers Weekly. Telling* is 12-year-old Cassie's story of being sexually molested by the father of the children she baby-sits.

Both *Detour for Emmy* and *Too Soon for Jeff* were selected by the American Library Association for its **Best Books for Young Adults List.**

Reynolds balances her time between writing, working with high school students, and keeping her back yard bird feeder filled. Her students help her keep in touch with the realities of today's teens, realities which are readily apparent in her novels.

She lives in Southern California with her husband, Mike. They are the parents of three grown children, Sharon, Cindi, and Matt, and the grandparents of Ashley and Kerry.

Laura Manriquez provided the lovely illustrations for *Beyond Dreams.*

OTHER RESOURCES FROM MORNING GLORY PRESS

DETOUR FOR EMMY. Novel about teenage pregnancy.

TOO SOON FOR JEFF. Novel from teen father's perspective.

TELLING. Novel about sexual molestation of 12-year-old.

TEENAGE COUPLES—Caring, Commitment and Change: How to Build a Relationship that Lasts. TEENAGE COUPLES— Coping with Reality: Dealing with Money, In-Laws, Babies and Other Details of Daily Life. Two books to help teenage couples develop healthy, loving and lasting relationships.

TEENS PARENTING—Your Pregnancy and Newborn Journey How to take care of yourself and your newborn. For pregnant teens. Available in "regular" (RL 6), Easier Reading (RL 3), and Spanish.

TEENS PARENTING—Your Baby's First Year
TEENS PARENTING—The Challenge of Toddlers
TEENS PARENTING—Discipline from Birth to Three
Three how-to-parent books especially for teenage parents.

VIDEO: "Discipline from Birth to Three" supplements above book.

TEEN DADS: Rights, Responsibilities and Joys. Parenting book for teenage fathers.

SURVIVING TEEN PREGNANCY: Choices, Dreams, Decisions For all pregnant teens—help with decisions, moving on toward goals.

SCHOOL-AGE PARENTS: The Challenge of Three-Generation Living. Help for families when teen daughter (or son) has a child.

BREAKING FREE FROM PARTNER ABUSE. Guidance for victims of domestic violence.

DID MY FIRST MOTHER LOVE ME? A Story for an Adopted Child. Birthmother shares her reasons for placing her child.

DO I HAVE A DADDY? A Story About a Single-Parent Child Picture/story book especially for children with only one parent. Also available in Spanish, *¿Yo tengo papá?*

PARENTS, PREGNANT TEENS AND THE ADOPTION OPTION. For parents of teens considering an adoption plan..

PREGNANT TOO SOON: Adoption Is an Option. Written to pregnant teens who may be considering an adoption plan.

ADOPTION AWARENESS: A Guide for Teachers, Counselors, Nurses and Caring Others. How to talk about adoption when no one is interested.

TEEN PREGNANCY CHALLENGE, Book One: Strategies for Change; Book Two: Programs for Kids. Practical guidelines for developing adolescent pregnancy prevention and care programs.

MORNING GLORY PRESS

6595 San Haroldo Way, Buena Park, CA 90620
714/828-1998 — FAX 714/828-2049

Please send me the following:

		Price	Total
__*Beyond Dreams*	Paper, ISBN 1-885356-00-5	8.95	_____
___	Cloth, ISBN 1-885356-01-3	15.95	_____
__*Too Soon for Jeff*	Paper, ISBN 0-930934-91-1	8.95	_____
___	Cloth, ISBN 0-930934-90-3	15.95	_____
__*Detour for Emmy*	Paper, ISBN 0-930934-76-8	8.95	_____
___	Cloth, ISBN 0-930934-75-x	15.95	_____
__*Telling*	Paper, ISBN 1-885356-03-x	8.95	_____
___	Cloth, ISBN 1-885356-04-8	15.95	_____
Teenage Couples: Caring, Commitment and Change			_____
___	Paper, ISBN 0-930934-93-8	9.95	_____
___	Cloth, ISBN 0-930934-92-x	15.95	_____
Teenage Couples: Coping with Reality			
___	Paper, ISBN 0-930934-86-5	9.95	_____
___	Cloth, ISBN 0-930934-87-3	15.95	_____
__*Teen Dads*	Paper, ISBN 0-930934-78-4	9.95	_____
___	Cloth, ISBN 0-930934-77-6	15.95	_____
__*Do I Have a Daddy?*	Cloth, ISBN 0-930934-45-8	12.95	_____
__*Did My First Mother Love Me?* ISBN 0-930934-85-7		12.95	_____
__*Breaking Free from Partner Abuse* 0-930934-74-1		7.95	_____
__*Surviving Teen Pregnancy* Paper, 0-930934-47-4		9.95	_____
School-Age Parents: Three-Generation Living			
___	Paper, ISBN 0-930934-36-9	10.95	_____
Teens Parenting—Your Pregnancy and Newborn Journey			
___	Paper, ISBN 0-930934-50-4	9.95	_____
Spanish—*Adolescentes como padres—La jornada . . .*			
___	Paper, ISBN 0-930934-69-5	9.95	_____
Teens Parenting—Your Baby's First Year			
___	Paper, ISBN 0-930934-52-0	9.95	_____
___	Cloth, ISBN 0-930934-53-9	15.95	_____
Teens Parenting—Challenge of Toddlers			
___	Paper, ISBN 0-930934-58-x	9.95	_____
___	Cloth, ISBN 0-930934-59-8	15.95	_____
Teens Parenting—Discipline from Birth to Three			
___	Paper, ISBN 0-930934-54-7	9.95	_____
___	Cloth, ISBN 0-930934-55-5	15.95	_____
__**VIDEO:** "Discipline from Birth to Three"		195.00	_____

TOTAL _____

Please add postage: 10% of total—Min., \$3.00   _____
California residents add 7.75% sales tax

TOTAL _____

Ask about quantity discounts, Teacher, Student Guides.
Prepayment requested. School/library purchase orders accepted.
If not satisfied, return in 15 days for refund.

NAME _____

ADDRESS _____